# MY VIKING WOLF

## A HOWLS VIKING ROMANCE

### GWEN KNIGHT

Copyright © 2017 by Gwen Knight

All rights reserved.

No part of this book may be reproduced in any form or by any electronic or mechanical means, including information storage and retrieval systems, without written permission from the author, except for the use of brief quotations in a book review.

 Created with Vellum

*I had a lot of fun writing in the Howls Romance project. Were it not for certain people, this book never would have happened. So, thank you to the creator of the Howls Romance project, and C.E. Black for inviting me into it. Thanks also go to Jori Buchanan for her dedication to editing this book, along with Debbie Herbert and R.E. Butler for offering to take time out of their own busy schedules to beta read.*

# My Viking Wolf

*How to Ruin Your Wedding Day: 101*
1. *Wake up in a stranger's bed.*
2. *Learn he's an assassin hired to kill you.*
3. *Fall in love with said assassin.*
4. *Kill rat-bastard fiancé.*

Reagan Compton trusts two things in life: her pack and her blade. Love never once registered on her radar. Until she meets the *shadow wolf*--a Viking assassin hired by her so-called fiancé to kill her. Luckily, he's more interested in claiming her for himself. Falling for her hired assassin wasn't a part of her life plans, but he's changing her mind *fast*. Love isn't easy, but it beats the hell out of death.

# 1

*THAT HAS to be the biggest dick I've ever seen...*

I raised a brow and stared down at the massive thing, all thick and brown and filled with creamy goodness. They expected me to fit the entire thing in my mouth? Yeah, right. Seemed more likely I'd go down as the first woman to die choking on a dick. Cause of death: cock. Was that even a thing?

We were about to find out.

"Oh, come *on* already," someone shouted over the thumping music.

I waved a dismissive hand, then rubbed my chin as I contemplated the task at hand. *One big swallow. Just open your mouth, stuff it in, and ride it out. Oh, and try not to embarrass yourself.* I rolled my eyes. I honestly couldn't see a way around that—considering the objective.

"Hurry up, woman!"

"Hold your damn horses," I shouted back.

This sort of thing required extreme concentration, and I only had one go at this. If I failed, I had to face the consequences.

All right. Now or never.

I spread my knees beneath me and clasped my hands behind my back. Then I bent at the waist, closed my eyes, and took the plunge. My lips slid down the length and the sweet flavor of chocolate cake and vanilla icing danced across my tongue. *Mmm, delicious.* Far more tasty than the real thing.

"Come on, Reagan!" My best friend, Lucy, shouted. Didn't matter that we were opponents in this competition, she still cheered me on. "Deeper, girl! Deeper!"

I snorted around the phallic-shaped cake. *Oh, God. Don't laugh! Focus on winning.*

The tip of the chocolate dick brushed the back of my throat, reminding me of my limits. This was as far as I went. I unleashed the chompers and bit right through the engorged width. Vanilla icing exploded in my mouth and coated my tongue. I moaned and started chewing, enjoying the scrumptious treat. Why couldn't every cock taste this good?

I dropped back onto my haunches, savoring every bit of the triple chocolate fudge cake. Kudos to the baker. She'd balanced the weight of the cake with the perfect amount of icing to help it slide down the throat.

Once I swallowed, I shot to my feet and punched my fist into the air with a loud cheer. I'd done it! I'd tackled the blow-job cake challenge without any embarrassing choking or slobbering on myself.

"Yeah!" I shouted, riling up my girlfriends.

A few of them threw back their heads and unleashed a chorus of high-pitched howls. Grinning, I thrust my other fist up into the air and howled with them. Every woman here belonged to my pack. When one howled, we all howled. Though, our deafening cheers seemed to attract unwanted attention.

In all the excitement, I hadn't noticed how quickly the club had filled up. We'd first arrived before the bouncers had even opened the doors, but as members of the great North American Pack, we always received a royal welcome no matter where we went. The club had only been too happy to host the impromptu bachelorette party Lucy had drummed up for me. Any werewolf publicity markedly increased their clientele, especially when the Reagan Compton and Benjamin Mathers wedding was all anyone could talk about.

We'd sequestered ourselves in the VIP section—as per the owner's instructions—and had soon devolved into the type of debauchery expected when dealing with rowdy werewolves. But it seemed the rest of the city had similar plans. The thrumming crowd pressed against the red velvet rope as the place practically burst at the seams. Hundreds of humans and werewolves alike stood on the other side of the rope, watching with amusement as we each lined up in front of our own dick-cake.

"Don't get too excited, hot shot," Lucy shouted over the music, her voice dragging me back to the competition. "I still have a turn."

Which, in layman's terms, meant I was fucked. As her best friend, I'd been subjected to every single one of her kinky stories—from the men she took home from clubs like this, to any coworkers she'd taken for a test-drive. On the scale of sexiness, she rated *femme fatale*, while I was little more than a blip on the radar. And I was all right with that. As the heir to my father's werewolf pack, I didn't have time to contemplate men or the art of seduction. It was my job to protect the pack. While Lucy had been out perfecting her flirting, I'd attended combat training.

I could kill a werewolf a dozen different ways in under a minute, but Lucy knew how to swallow more dick than anyone I knew.

With a saucy wink, she pulled back her long blonde hair and dropped to her knees in front of the cake. As part of the bachelorette party, the women in my pack had decided it'd be fun to try this challenge. Whoever bit off the largest chunk won the game. Thankfully, they'd opted for cake as opposed to bananas or carrots. I was getting married, I wasn't dead. I'd take cake over fruits and vegetables any day of the week.

Lucy barely took a breath before she bent over and engulfed the cake. I swear to God, her lips brushed the base where the bakers had cleverly crafted two chocolate balls. No doubt about it—Lucy had won. I only hoped she didn't choke, but she downed that cake like a pro.

A raucous swell of laughter rose above the music. The girls all jogged over to me and patted my back.

"Good try!"

But before I could respond, two others sauntered over

with three martini glasses in hand. As expected, the consequences were shots. And Lucy, as the organizer of this event, had chosen the most embarrassing one she could imagine: the Muff Diver.

She handed me the long-stemmed glass topped with an excessive amount of whipped cream and giggled. "Bottoms up, Reagan!"

*Bottoms up, indeed.* I should have expected this.

Sighing, I grasped the bottom of the glass, the only part I was allowed to touch, and shoved my face into the cream, careful not to inhale. After a few moments of blindly rooting around, my lips closed around the shot glass. I lifted my head and tipped it back, the thick liquor pouring down my throat.

"Woo!" Lucy shouted. "A pro over here!"

I plucked the shot glass out of my mouth and slammed it down on the counter. "There! Now, get me something real to drink."

Chuckling, Lucy handed me a chilled bottle of beer. "Already did."

Ah, she knew me so well.

I grabbed the nearest napkin and wiped my face clean. A part of me feared asking what she had in store next. Lord only knew with Lucy. I loved her spontaneous and carefree nature, even though it often landed me in situations like these. Hand me a dagger or a sword, and I was unstoppable. But Lucy was fearless, even when faced with the most terrifying things. Like love.

Thankfully, I never needed to worry about that.

Loving Benjamin Mathers wasn't on my to-do list. Our upcoming nuptials were nothing more than a political maneuver. A means of joining his European pack to our American one. It was an arranged marriage, but Lucy had insisted I still deserved the same treatment as any other bride.

A familiar rhythm thumped through the club's impressive speaker system. I knew it was Lucy's favorite song the moment she squealed, snatched my hand, and wrenched me out onto the dance floor where a writhing mass of sweaty bodies awaited us. Lucy ruthlessly plowed her way through the crowd until she found the best spot *right* next to the speakers. I could barely hear a thing above the heavy beat vibrating beneath my feet. Not that it mattered. Lucy wanted to *move*, not talk.

She swayed to the music, her eyes already closed as she lost herself to the sound. I wasn't as quick to give in to the rhythm. Someone's thigh brushed against mine, while another woman pressed herself flush against my back. Unknown fingers caressed my hips and slid up to my waist. I'd been trained to fight at close combat, but this was more than I'd bargained for.

*Ah, screw it.* Tonight was my bachelorette party. And even though the marriage was a sham, I still wanted to go out with a bang. Forget my hang-ups and simply lose myself to the music. Drink to my heart's content. Eat cake and be merry. All the things I typically didn't engage in.

I moved in time with Lucy, swaying to the familiar melodies and heavy bass. When one song ended, we moved seamlessly into the next. Our admirers came and went, their bodies a constant reminder that we weren't alone. I'd stopped caring, though. For one night, I intended to forget all my worries and enjoy the here and now.

After the umpteenth song, I tapped the back of Lucy's hand and gestured toward my empty beer, drained as we'd danced. Then I pointed to the bar. She nodded and we shuffled our way out of the throng.

Perhaps a tad more blitzed than she'd let on, Lucy tripped on the last step. She laughed as she toppled into me, her hands gripping my arms. For a moment, I knew this was it. We were going down like the proverbial Titanic.

Until I felt my back collide into someone else.

"Hey!" Rough hands shoved me from behind. "Watch where you're going!"

I turned, ready to apologize. But as I pivoted, my hand knocked his beer from his hand. It fell to the ground, the glass shattering and spilling booze all over his shoes.

"You kiddin' me?" he shouted.

Lucy gripped my arm and circled around me. "Sorry about that! My fault. I stumbled into her."

"Stupid bitch," he snarled.

I gave a slow blink and lifted my gaze until I caught his bloodshot eyes. "Now, is that any way to speak to us? She apologized."

The asshat contemplated me with a pursed mouth, clearly wondering how far to push this. Not only were we women, but werewolves, too. And every last person in the joint knew it. With the throng of people surrounding us, I couldn't pick up on his scent. But I would have bet my last dollar he was human.

Sometimes that worked in our favor, sometimes it didn't.

When he straightened to his full height and stepped closer to me, I knew this would be one of *those* moments.

"You owe me a beer," he rasped in my face, his breath rank. "Bitch."

I caught movement from the corner of my eye—the bouncer ready to jump to our aid. I lifted a hand and shook my head. "You know, I really don't like that word. I'm not a dog, and I'm not in heat."

He quirked a grin. "Then buy me a beer and we'll call us square."

The logical part of my brain told me to do it. Cave to his demand, spend the seven dollars, and walk away. But damn it if the other half wasn't itching to put him in his place. Lucy had apologized, after all. Maybe he needed to be taught some manners.

"Reagan, don't," Lucy shouted, her fingers digging into my arm.

See—she knew me well. She didn't even need to see my face to know the thoughts running through my head.

"It's not worth it. We're here to have fun."

Sometimes fighting *was* fun. A rush of adrenaline, a release of tension—almost as satisfying as an orgasm. But Lucy was right. Tonight wasn't about fighting. She'd brought me here to celebrate, and I didn't want to ruin that.

Holding the shithead's gaze, I slipped my hand into my back pocket, fished out a crisp new ten dollar bill, and slapped it against his chest. "Here you go, big guy."

The second I turned away, I caught the distinct

sound of his voice. Pros and cons of preternatural hearing. Had I been human, I might not have heard him above the racket.

"Pussy-ass werewolf."

I froze, my pulse drumming in my ears.

"Reagan, no," Lucy shouted. "He's drunk. He's just being an ass to show off for his buddies."

I knew that. I really did. But my years as one of the highest-ranked wolves in North America had taught me one thing. You never walk away from a challenge. This fucknugget was human—but that didn't change anything. He wanted to prove he was better than me, stronger, more dominant.

He didn't stand a chance.

"Reagan, please..."

With a sweet grin, I turned back toward him. "You know, on second thought..." I plucked the ten dollar bill from his hand before he could so much as blink. "I think I'm going to use this on another round of drinks for me and my friend here. You know, your way of apologizing for being such a prick."

His gaze dropped to his hand and his face purpled. "Hey! That's mine!"

I unleashed the alpha stare I'd perfected many moons ago. "Then come and get it."

He hesitated, a flicker of unease shadowing his face. His focus darted to his buddies, as though wondering whether or not he should push any harder. I could have told him not to bother, but some decisions people had to make for themselves.

"Keep it," he grumbled after wisely assuming I'd wipe the floor with him.

I flashed him a smile. "Thanks!"

"Yeah, whatever." He turned away, subjecting himself to his friends' jeers.

"You didn't have to do that," Lucy called over the music.

I shot her a droll look. Yes, I did. I was Reagan Compton—daughter of Gabriel Compton, the alpha of the North American Pack. And I was his heir. Putting people in their place was my job.

"Come on, I'll buy the next round," I told her, waving the money in front of her face.

The moment she cracked a smile, I knew she'd forgiven me. Booze and men—the surest ways to Lucy's heart. And I loved her dearly for it.

We sidled up alongside the bar, about to order our drinks when someone caught Lucy's eye. *Flirt mode activated*, I chuckled to myself. I gestured for my own fresh drink when a single shot slid my way. The glass glided over the wooden counter and came to a stop right next to my hand. Impressive. Not a drop spilled.

I glanced over, expecting to reject the offer, but found myself stunned into silence instead. There leaning against the counter was a man I could only describe as *sex on a stick*. Jesus. The wavy dark hair, the piercing blue eyes...everything a guy needed to make the ladies swoon. Which, I would never—not in a million years—even if my legs did feel a little wobbly. It didn't help that I'd always had a thing for chiseled jaws, and man-candy here seemed to be carved from stone itself.

"For you," he said, his voice much deeper than I'd expected.

I eyed him up, drinking in the sinfully fitted jeans and white t-shirt that strained across his shoulders. *Just...wow.* I'd never been struck speechless by the sight of a man before. Then again, I'd never met the living embodiment of a wet dream before. Not that it mattered. The wedding was tomorrow. My single days were numbered.

When I didn't immediately respond, he quirked a crooked grin, one that drew my attention to his mouth. The slightest scar slashed his upper lip—a curious thing since werewolves rarely scarred. And he was definitely *all* werewolf. It didn't matter that we were surrounded by a massive crowd of sweaty bodies—I could smell his wolf. His unique scent teased my senses until I couldn't smell anything else. It stirred my wolf, beckoning her out of the darkness as though waking her from a deep slumber.

"Well?" Hottie with a Body asked, gesturing toward the glass.

I should have shook my head, told him I was spoken for, and handed back the shot. But was I spoken for at this very moment? Until I said my vows, I wasn't tied to anyone. Hell, I'd only met Benjamin once. And in that time, I'd never made any promises.

*And it's only a drink...*

Ah, the devil on my shoulder come to play.

I waited for the other, quieter voice to kick in—the one insisting I smarten up and remember my commitments. Except, it never spoke up, and the devil continued to whisper provocative little thoughts in my ear. What was one drink in the grand scheme of things? One final night to enjoy a little flirtation.

So, with a wicked grin, I picked up the shot, toasted the gorgeous man, and tossed it down the hatch.

The devil was a conniving little bastard.

THE ALCOHOL BURNED as it slid down my throat. Tears welled in my eyes, and I laughed as I coughed against the back of my hand. I hadn't bothered to check the shot before downing it. Not that it would have mattered. The entire point was to embrace tonight and all that came my way—to enjoy myself one last time before signing my freedom away to a political marriage. And if that meant drinking tequila, so be it.

"A bit strong?"

I flicked Mr. Hottie next to me a watery glance and grinned. "A lime might have helped."

Without a word, he reached behind the counter and fished out a small container brimming with a mixture of lemons and limes. He set it down next to me and gestured toward the fruit. I grabbed the top lime and popped it into my mouth, my lashes fluttering as the burn subsided.

"Thanks," I said with a smile.

He nodded toward the dance floor. "I saw you out there."

Shame burned through my cheeks. Dancing wasn't one of my talents. "Oh, yeah? Enjoy watching someone flop around like a fish out of water?"

Desire flashed in his eyes. "Trust me, there wasn't any flopping."

I ducked my head, then peered up at him from beneath my lashes. "Well, thank you for saying that."

"But I wasn't referring to your dancing. I meant with Joe the Asshole over there."

I bit back a laugh. Joe the Asshole. I liked that. I'd definitely need to remember that when retelling the story. I glanced over my shoulder at the group of unruly boys. Thankfully, a new round of drinks had distracted them from me and Lucy, but it didn't stop them from leering at other women—some from my pack.

My eyes narrowed as I watched the unfolding scene. A bit handsy, but nothing my packmates couldn't handle. It took every bit of willpower to keep me from stalking back over there and cuffing Joe upside the back of the head. But I had to trust my packmates would handle it. As a rule of thumb, every single member of the pack knew how to fight. I'd long since eschewed the traditional dominant versus submissive concept that most werewolves practiced. Every single member had a duty to train alongside the rest of us, whether or not they were born warriors. We were only as strong as our weakest member. Surprisingly, some of the weaker members had shown a real affinity for the training, and I'd been lucky to watch them grow into something so much more than they'd ever thought possible.

Marie—as an example—was one of our younger members. But when Joe the Asshole caressed her rear, she grabbed him by the fingers and snapped his hand backward. That quickly, he dropped to a knee, cursing so loudly I could hear him above the music.

"I was going to offer some help with him," the hottie next to me said, "but I think you all have it handled."

"Thanks, though. I appreciate the thought."

"Safe to say he's having a bad night."

Laughing, I tore my focus away from Joe the Asshole and turned back to Mr. Bedroom Eyes. I needed a better name for him. Definitely couldn't spend the night thinking of him as sexual euphemisms. *Or can I?* Nawh... probably not the best idea.

"So, you have a name?" I asked.

The right corner of his mouth twitched. "Jerrik."

"Jerrik," I repeated, testing it out for myself. "Interesting name. Sort of Old World." Which didn't mean much when dealing with werewolves, considering our long lifespans.

He inclined his head toward me, his eyes catching the strobe lights. I felt like I should recognize him. Like the world should have somehow made me aware of his existence before now.

"Don't you want to know who I am?" I asked.

"I already know who you are, Reagan. Every werewolf in North America knows who you are."

Fair point.

And quite true. For the past five hundred years, my father had led the pack. Because of him, they'd sailed from Europe to the New World to establish a new colony, one free from their last alpha's oppressive rule. Those who had followed my father had pledged their undying loyalty to him—a loyalty that existed to this day. Lucy often joked about my family. *Werewolf royalty*, she called us. I didn't know of every werewolf, but they certainly knew of me. Especially considering I was the one slotted to take over the pack whenever my father decided to pass it on.

Jerrik slid closer, closing the distance between us.

I bit back a grin. I couldn't help it. I liked that he seemed interested in me. Part of me wished he didn't know who I was, but what were the chances of that? I couldn't go anywhere without someone recognizing me, human or werewolf alike, thanks to the media. The humans loved sticking their noses in our business.

"Every eye in this place is on you, did you know that?" he asked, his voice carrying over the pounding music.

I didn't bother to look. "That's normal for me."

"Did you know they call you the *Werewolf Princess*?"

I cringed. "Not a title I particularly enjoy."

"Why not?"

"Because it gives the wrong impression. It makes me sound soft."

"Ah." He grinned at me. "And nothing like the warrior you are."

I tilted my head and regarded him. "You sure do seem to know a lot about me."

"While you seem to know nothing about me."

"I feel like I should apologize for that," I said, laughing. The only thing I knew about him was he was drop-dead gorgeous. And at the moment, that was all I wanted to know.

He crossed his arms over his chest and gave me a once-over. "Trust me, there's no need. I prefer it that way."

I grinned at him. "Prefer to remain mysterious, do you?"

"Almost exclusively."

"But I know your name now," I pointed out. "A few clicks on my phone, and I'll know everything there is to know about you."

"That so? And what is it you think you'll find?"

"Facebook?" I said. "Twitter?"

He shook his head. "Not a social media kind of guy."

"Really." My interest officially peaked. "No hidden websites? No Tinder account?"

"Certainly not."

"Hey, it's the newest craze. You really should get with the times."

He leaned against the bar, his legs crossed at the ankles. "And what about you? Any secret websites or fake dating profiles?"

I shook my head, my cheeks starting to burn from smiling so much. "Doesn't seem wise. I'm in the spotlight enough without adding fuel to the fire."

He shot a glance to my empty beer and without asking, waved the bartender over. "Two more."

Lucy brushed against my side and caught my eye. She silently gestured toward Jerrik, her brows lifted in appreciation before she mouthed the words *he's hot* at me. I bit back a grin. I didn't need her to point that out. I had eyes. She threw me a wink before returning to whoever she'd struck up a conversation with. I hadn't bothered to look, a tad distracted as it were.

The bartender dropped two chilled bottles down before us. I thanked him, popped the cap, and took a heartening sip.

"So, I'm pretty sure I've never seen you here before," Jerrik commented.

"Only pretty sure?" I teased.

"All right. I *know* I've never seen you here."

I canted my head to the side and laughed. "And how would you know that?"

He eased another bit closer, our shoulders now touching. "Because I would have noticed you."

His words sent a wave of heat through my stomach. Feeling brave, I held my position instead of backing away. I liked the feel of him against me and secretly longed for more. "You do seem the observant type. Tell me something, Jerrik. When did you first notice me tonight? While dealing with Joe the Asshole, on the dance floor, or..." I gestured toward the VIP section. "Back there?"

He lifted his beer and took a long sip, a means of hiding a grin, I suspected. "Truthfully? Back there."

I groaned. Figured he'd noticed us while shoving

inches of cake down our throats. "Then, the observant guy that you are, did you figure out why we're here?"

His head bobbed. "Celebrating your bachelorette party. I think everyone in the club knows."

I shot him a stunned glance. "So...you don't care that I'm getting married tomorrow?"

His bright blue eyes slammed into mine, and I swear the world around us sizzled. I felt my temperature rise and my breath quicken. He held my gaze, his dark lashes rising and falling with every blink. After a moment's pause, he licked his lips, and asked, "Do you?"

His sensuous voice sent a shiver down my spine. I forced myself to swallow and shook my head. "Not at the moment."

"Good." He took the beer from me and set it on the counter next to his. Then he extended his hand. "Shall we?"

"Shall we...?"

But he didn't answer. Instead, he took my hand and led me out onto the dance floor. Halfway there, I glanced back to find Lucy watching me, her brows raised in shock. A part of me wanted to dash back to her side and ask her advice. I'd never actually danced with a man before. And I highly doubted sparring was considered the same thing.

I gestured toward Jerrik, my panic communicating my thoughts.

*Go!* She mouthed. *Dance!*

A sharp tug on my hand whirled me around. I stumbled forward, my hands landing against his chest—his *hard as rock* chest. Wow. He hooked a finger under my chin and lifted until our eyes met, then started to move in time to the music. I couldn't resist. I slid my hands around his neck just as he grasped my hips. His touch sent a wave of heat through me, and without thinking, I stepped closer until our bodies touched. With a panty-melting grin, he wrapped his arms around my waist, the palm of his hand searing the small of my back.

Jesus, he knew how to dance. His every move provoked a naughty thought, tempting me to jump his bones right here and now. And from the smell of it, I knew he wouldn't mind. His arousal possessed a heady note, entirely intoxicating as I breathed it in. It teased my senses, and sparked a desire unlike anything I'd ever felt. Surprising, considering I'd known him for all of five minutes. That didn't matter to my body, though.

The song changed, but we didn't stop dancing, didn't change tempo to keep up with the beat. Our bodies moved in rhythm, taking every possible opportunity to brush against one another. He made my head spin, and my heart race.

I unlinked my hands and pressed my palm against his chest. His heart hammered against his ribs, matching my own quickened pace. I lifted my head and met his gaze, our mouths inches apart. I desperately wanted to feel his lips against mine, but I couldn't. Not here.

Was the booze affecting my head? I'd drunk quite a bit throughout the night. But somehow, I didn't think that was it. No one else here held my attention like he did. No one else called to my wolf. I felt her in the back of my mind, anxiously watching, waiting for one of us to make the first move.

I wanted it to be him. Wanted him to pull me up against him and claim my mouth. Startling, to feel so strongly for someone I'd only just met. Yet, it felt right. Him holding me as we danced...there wasn't anything that felt *wrong* about it.

He leaned closer. So close that I thought he might kiss me right here in front of everyone. Instead, his lips brushed along my jaw and found my ear. I shivered in his arms and bared my neck, my eyes fluttering shut when his hot breath caressed my throat.

"Wanna get out of here?" he murmured.

*Hell, yes!* But could I? My upcoming wedding was nothing more than a political alliance—we all knew that. My father and Benjamin's father, Christian, were old friends from back in the day. And now that Christian wanted to bring his pack west, they'd agreed to join us all through marriage, to ease the transition, expand the pack, and avoid any unnecessary territorial fights. Benjamin and I had only met once, and nothing about him had inspired anything within me. Not like Jerrik. His touch made me burn.

When I didn't immediately respond, Jerrik lifted a hand to my shoulder and brushed his fingers along my neck. The simplest caress, but one that turned me to putty in his hands.

"Reagan..." he growled in my ear.

*Oh, God.* The sound of his rumbling voice.

Tonight was the last night of my single life. I'd made no promises to Benjamin. No agreements to remain celibate before the wedding. And I wanted Jerrik like no one else. I *knew* I needed to feel him above me. Even if only for one night. And in the back of my mind, my wolf agreed.

His hand tightened on my waist, and he brushed his lips against the curve of my bare shoulder. "I'm gonna need an answer, dove."

"Yes," I whispered, internally swooning at the sound of his pet name.

He lifted his head, his face partially hidden in shadow, but his eyes brighter than ever. "Yes?"

I nodded. "Get me out of here."

"As my lady commands," he murmured.

He took my hand and led me off the dance floor. I swept the bar in search of Lucy, but couldn't find her. And I didn't want to waste any time seeking her out. Jerrik snatched a leather jacket off the back of a chair as we passed by and led me toward the door. I followed, my nerves buzzing. I couldn't believe I was doing this, but I knew this was where I wanted to be tonight.

Once outside, he draped his jacket over my shoulders and pointed to his motorcycle with a lifted brow. "You sure about this?"

To dispel any doubts, I climbed astride the leather seat. "You coming?"

"I sure hope so." He threw me an impish grin, then seated himself in front of me and revved the engine. With a loud roar, we took off into the darkness with my arms wrapped around his waist and his bike vibrating between my thighs.

Tonight's goal was new experiences. In the span of an hour, I'd ticked two items off a bucket list that hadn't previously existed. *Leave with a perfect stranger, and ride a motorcycle.* Good progress for a single night's work, with hopefully more to come. Before now, I'd never tried anything new. I'd been content with my lot in life, training and readying myself to take over the pack. As the heir, it was my duty to obey my father's every command. And I'd done so without complaint. I'd never taken a moment to consider anything else. Never done anything I knew he would disapprove of.

Until now.

Going home with a random man the night before my wedding certainly ranked in the top five worst decisions I'd ever made, but I didn't care. Not one bit. Tomorrow I would walk down the aisle and pledge myself to someone

I barely knew. I would do my duty to the pack and to my father. So I deserved this. One night to cut loose and have fun, and make my own choices—even horrible ones.

Oddly enough, Jerrik didn't feel like a bad decision. Nor did he feel random. Right now, pressed up against him with my hands brushing his sides and my thighs pressed against his hips...I felt like I'd always known him. Like I'd been waiting my entire life for this one moment.

A moment I refused to waste.

Pushing those heavy thoughts to the back of my mind, I threw my arms out to the side and tipped my head back. The wind combed through my hair and rushed over my face, the notion of freedom overtaking me. I'd never felt such an adrenaline rush before, not even when leading my men into battle. My entire body hummed with excitement, every knotted nerve alight with newfound energy. I never wanted it to end.

"How you doing back there?" Jerrik shouted over the roar of the engine.

A wide grin spread across my face. I sat up and debated how to respond. If tonight was our only night, I didn't want to waste a second of it. I wanted to experience this thing called life I'd been missing out on.

Jerrik slowed to take a curve. I tightened my grip around his waist and pressed my face against his back, my hands splayed across his stomach. I could feel the top of his belt buckle brushing against my fingers, tempting me to dip that little bit lower. A hot stab of excitement pooled between my legs as I tinkered with the idea of sliding my hand into his pants. But I wasn't quite ready for that. Those were Lucy-esque moves.

Instead, I placed my hands on his shoulders and stood, balancing on the footrests. Jerrik's body stiffened and he snuck a quick glance my way before turning back to the road. I slid my hand down his arm and pulled it away from the handlebar, then swung my leg around to the front. He moved with me, repositioning himself as I sat down in front of him, my back to the road and my legs wrapped around his waist.

Jerrik laughed, a rich sound that gave me goosebumps. "You sure you want to sit there?"

*Oh, yeah.* Maybe it was reckless, but I didn't care. Advantage to being a werewolf. We could take risks humans couldn't.

He shifted gears and the bike started to slow. Curious, I glanced over my shoulder and spotted a red light. Though the roads were empty, and only a few stragglers occupied the sidewalks, he still came to a complete stop.

"You seem to be having fun," Jerrik commented.

Fun didn't begin to describe it. I felt *alive*. I dragged my gaze up his chest, my mouth watering at the sight of that perfect jaw and the sensuous curve of his mouth. There was something I'd wanted to do since we'd met, and with my heart skipping in my chest and my hair tousled from the wind, now seemed like the perfect moment.

Before I talked myself out of it, I grabbed him by the shirt and pulled him down. Our mouths came together, and my whole world exploded. I sucked in a sharp breath and parted my lips, a rush of desire blazing through my chest when his tongue brushed mine, teasing me with his maddeningly slow strokes.

He growled and pulled me against him, the leather seat digging into my ass. Not that I cared. Nothing in the world could have convinced me to stop. I'd instigated the kiss, but he'd taken full control, his mouth hard and demanding, yet so wickedly talented. He nipped at my bottom lip, feeding at my mouth. I responded with equal abandon, my fingers spearing into his hair as I held on for dear life.

A horn blasted through the air behind us. I jumped and broke from the kiss, my hand flying to my tender mouth.

Jerrik ignored the second honk and instead stared down at me, his eyes burning with golden light. "Jesus. Where the hell have you been my whole life?"

Warmth spread through my cheeks, but before I could answer, he kicked the bike back into drive and shot through the intersection.

I couldn't concentrate the rest of the ride. My only thought was getting off this bike and finishing what we'd started. I wanted so much more than that small taste. I wanted everything.

He finally pulled into a driveway and parked the bike. My abused ears rang as we climbed off, but I still heard him mutter *thank fuck*. He grabbed my hand and tugged me up the stairs. I barely had a chance to admire the front porch before we staggered through the door. We laughed as I tripped over a pair of discarded boots, but Jerrik didn't bother to move them. Instead, he hoisted me up onto his hips and pressed me flat against the wall. His mouth found mine while his hands slid under my shirt and explored the curves of my body.

Too many clothes.

I wanted him naked and above me, or below me. I didn't much care which. But it needed to happen, and now. Dizzy with anticipation, my fingers and toes tingled with desire. Heat exploded in my stomach when his fingers brushed my nipples, and my pulse kicked into overdrive when he tugged my shirt off.

Hoping not to be left behind, I popped open his buttons and slid his shirt down his arms, pausing to admire the ripped muscles I'd *known* were hidden beneath. I whistled an appreciative tune under my breath and eyed every inch of him. My own personal Adonis. The broad shoulders, the defined pecs, and the fine dusting of dark hair that disappeared into his jeans. All of him, simply perfect.

And I needed more.

His hand cupped the back of my neck before he pulled me away from the wall and staggered through the house. We slammed into his bedroom, and toppled down onto his bed. I spared a breath to laugh, but Jerrik's mouth came down on mine, silencing me with a drugging kiss. I moaned against him and arched my body. His hand slipped around my back and removed my bra with a quick flick of his experienced fingers. Once bare to the cool air, his lips sealed around one of my nipples while his thumb brushed the other.

I cried out and reached for his belt, tearing it off in a single pull. His pants went next with me barely pausing to unbutton the fly. In the hurry to undress him, I'd hardly noticed him doing the same. It wasn't until I lay naked beneath him that I stopped for a breath.

*Holy shit.* This was happening. Like *actually* happening.

My nerves crept up on me, and my heart kicked against my ribs. I was about to experience my first one-night stand. At the ripe age of one hundred and two. A baby compared to most werewolves.

Sensing the change of direction in my thoughts, Jerrik lifted his head, his lips a touch swollen. "Reagan?"

Every doubt screamed in my head. What was I doing? Who was he? I didn't know a thing about him. But he knew everything about me. What if this was a game? A bet to see who could bed Reagan Compton? Thoughts I fought to silence. Worry about them later.

"Shh," he whispered. He lowered down and brushed his lips against mine.

"I've never done this before," I murmured, deciding honesty might be best in this situation. Better late than never.

His mouth curved into a half grin. "Then let me show you how."

*Yes, please.*

He slid down my body, his mouth coming to rest between my thighs. The moment his tongue stroked me, I whimpered and arched against him, my hips rising off the bed. Every lick was maddening, promising a climatic ending but never delivering. Every time I neared the edge, he pulled back, teasing me with the promise of something wonderful.

I thrust my fingers into his hair, begging him to finish what he started.

Jerrik slid a finger within me and moved in time with his tongue, teasing me both inside and out. The pleasure spiked, the warmth blooming within my stomach so suddenly that I cried out when my orgasm burst through me. Every inch of me reveled in the sensation and rode out the waves. Only then did I open my eyes to find Jerrik positioned between my thighs, his length already sheathed in a condom.

He lowered down and claimed my mouth in a demanding kiss that left me breathless. I felt him positioning himself, and when he slid inside me, I gasped, my hands digging into his muscled back. My body shuddered as I adjusted to his width. I wrapped my legs around him and lifted my hips, my head digging into the pillows when he started to move. He began a quick rhythm, his every thrust bringing me that much closer to the edge. Jerrik growled as he moved within me, his rhythm shattering as he thrust deeper and deeper. My hands gripped the sheets when the next orgasm tore through me, my body clenching around him. His head fell forward and he grunted as he finished, the tips of his hair brushing against my chest.

He collapsed next to me, equally breathless.

*Wow.* I didn't know what else to think, or if I was even capable of thinking. My head was a mush of erratic thoughts. Thankfully, none of which centered on regret.

After disposing of the condom, Jerrik reached out and pulled me close, resting my head in the nook between his chest and arm. I thought it'd feel weird, but it felt so right.

Startlingly and frighteningly right. The thought terrified me. Tomorrow was my wedding. Tonight was *not* the night to be tempted by the thought of finding something with a *different* man. I'd meant this to be an adventure, something to remember my single life by. One last crazy night before I took the step down marriage lane. But Jerrik didn't feel like a one-night stand type guy. And that was more than my befuddled brain could handle at the moment.

"You're like an open book," Jerrik murmured before he leaned down and brushed a kiss against my brow. "Stop thinking and just relax."

"Easier said than done," I whispered back. My thoughts were crazy loud. Annoyingly so.

He positioned himself until our gazes met. "Do you want to talk about it?"

*God, no.* These thoughts and fears were for my ears only. Besides, how could he help?

"I've been around a really long time," he said, answering my unspoken thought. "I've seen things, experienced things..."

"How long?" I asked, my curiosity piqued.

"Oh..." He released a heavy breath. "A while. Longer than most."

My brows furrowed. What did that mean? I pushed up onto my elbows. "Like three hundred years? Four?"

The right side of his mouth tugged upward. "Longer."

"Five?"

He exhaled and stretched onto his back.

Longer than five hundred years then. My father was

the oldest werewolf I knew at six-hundred-and-thirty years. Could Jerrik be older? The thought astounded me. I didn't know what to make of it. Generally speaking, werewolves didn't live past five hundred. Most chose to end their own lives, exhausted or driven mad by the world around them. My father was one of the few who'd made it past the big five-oh-oh, and I'd always believed it was pure stubbornness that kept him hanging around longer than others.

"Jerrik..."

He wrapped his arms around me and drew me back into his chest. "Sleep, dove. Tomorrow is a big day. You'll need all the rest you can get."

I caught a flicker of light in his eyes. A flash of gold lightning. Maybe it was my imagination, but it seemed like he didn't like the idea of tomorrow any more than I did.

Insane, right? We'd only just met.

"What if I don't want to sleep?" I whispered as I slid my hand over his toned stomach, my target just a little further south. My body still buzzed, orgasmic aftermath and all that. Sleep could wait.

Jerrik turned to me with a smirk. "You young'uns, always so eager."

I bit back a chuckle and cupped his length, my eyes widening when I found him fully erect.

With a growl, he rolled over and pinned me beneath his massive body. "I'm old. Not dead."

I couldn't help but laugh. A sound that quickly turned to a low moan when his hand snaked up my thigh.

Had to make this night count, right?

My eyes snapped open when something brushed against my chest. Blinded by sunlight, I had to blink a few times before my vision returned to normal, but when it did... *Sweet Jesus.* Nothing here belonged to me. The walls, the bed, the soft sheets pooled around my waist. Memories of last night came flooding back, and my heart practically flatlined. Images of Jerrik rushed forward, the feel of his breath against my skin, his hands against my body—the same hand now resting beneath the swell of my breast. I sucked in a sharp breath and glanced over at him, my gaze falling on the gorgeous bastard.

*Holy shit, holy shit, holy shit.*

I stared up at the ceiling and counted to one hundred and two in my head. One for every year of my stupid, stupid life. I'd *slept* with him. A complete stranger. The night before my wedding. That had to qualify as the dumbest move ever.

And to make things infinitely worse, I didn't want to leave his bed. Every bone in my body longed to remain right here, tucked into his side. Forget Benjamin and the treaty and my father. Maybe Jerrik and I could run away together...

*Stupid! Just shut up, right the fuck now.*

I had a duty. My pack depended on me. My *father* depended on me. Regardless of my desires, I needed to get out of bed right this second and vanish. Preferably *before* Jerrik woke.

Holding my breath, I slipped out from under the sheets and sat up, careful not to disturb him. I didn't want to deal with saying goodbye. He and I had both known upfront that this was nothing more than a fling. And for all I knew, he didn't want more. Maybe one-night stands were his thing. Maybe desperate and lonely women were his forte. Or, maybe I was a fool who had completely lost her mind.

That seemed legit.

Temporary insanity. I could swing it if anyone asked. Not that anyone would. As far as they knew, I'd ducked out before the end of the festivities. Before the end of my *own* bachelorette party. I swallowed a groan and dropped my head into my palms.

*God.* Lucy alone would badger me until I told her where I'd disappeared to. I needed an excuse, a lie. A headache? No, she'd seen me with Jerrik. *Shit.* This had just become all sorts of messy.

I stole a glance back at Jerrik. He looked so peaceful

and handsome in the morning sunlight, one hand stretched toward my side of the bed. The sheets had slipped down to his hips, teasing me with a glimpse of his rock-hard stomach. For five hundred—or older—he sure didn't look it. Not that many werewolves did. Physically, we stopped aging around thirty. Another upside to our supernatural genetics.

Fighting the temptation to curl up against him, I rose to my feet and started hunting down my clothes. In our rush to strip each other, he'd scattered my clothing all over the room. My bra hung haphazardly off a lamp, my underwear discarded in the middle of the floor. I grimaced at the thought of putting them back on, but thankfully, I knew fresh clothing awaited me at the church. Not to mention a very white dress I didn't want to wear.

I threw on my clothes and dug my phone out of my back pocket. Eight missed calls from Lucy. I ignored those and glanced at the time. Ten o'clock. I choked back a gasp. Two hours late. *Two fucking hours late!* To my own wedding, which started in an hour. Lucy was going to kill me.

I bolted out of the bedroom and dashed toward the front door, the whole time silently praying he didn't wake up. I reached for the doorknob and glanced back. No movement from Jerrik's room. Just the sound of his steady breath as he slept. I felt bad running out on him like this, but two hours late...I needed to leave, *now*. And the idiot I was, I'd let him drive me here last night. Wherever *here* was.

My monumental fuck up kept getting bigger.

I snuck outside and closed the door behind me before dashing down the stairs. Once on the street, I pulled my phone out and activated my location and the map feature. At least something had worked in my favor today. Jerrik lived about fifteen blocks away from the church.

*Thank God.*

Calling a cab would take time. And I knew I could run that distance in no time flat. I slid my phone back into my pocket and allowed myself one final glance at Jerrik's house. It didn't matter that every inch of me protested leaving. I had somewhere else to be. Right now.

With a final goodbye, I turned and started jogging through the streets.

---

I MADE it to the church with fifty minutes to spare. It'd taken some ruthless maneuvering, like bowling over two old ladies who had then scolded me in their quivering voices, and outrunning a dog who'd decided I was more interesting than his rubber ball, but I'd made it.

The church loomed up in front of me, all stained glass windows and judgemental stone reliefs. Religion and I did *not* get along, but that didn't stop me from wincing at the sight of the massive cross piercing the sky.

It wasn't infidelity if I hadn't spoken any vows yet, right? Not to mention, I'd barely met the groom. One brief exchange that hadn't left a memorable impression on me. The way I saw it, we weren't a couple until we stood before the priest and pledged ourselves to one another.

So…why did I feel so guilty? Doubtful anyone would care that I'd slept with someone else last night. For all I knew, Benjamin had done the same. A final farewell to our single lives.

All right. Time to get down to brass tacks. Virtue-wise, I stood in the clear. I'd broken no vows, and, most importantly, no laws…that I could remember. Therefore, the cross shouldn't evoke *any* morality issues. Thankfully, the actual wedding would be held in the gardens in the back due to the number of guests. I wouldn't have to tolerate the cross and religious motifs for long. Just while I dressed.

I smoothed my hands down my pants, and strode into the church. With every step, my heart beat a little bit faster and my palms broke into a clammy sweat. But I wouldn't forsake my duty. I'd promised my father I would marry Benjamin and cement the newly devised treaty. And I kept my promises.

"Oh my God. Reagan!"

Lucy's frantic voice echoed in my ears. I spun around and watched as she barrelled toward me in her maid-of-honor gown, a look of utter madness darkening her face.

"Where the fuck have you been? No! Never mind. I don't want to know! I've been trying to call you. You're *so* late. What happened to our plan to meet here at eight?"

At eight, I'd been asleep in Jerrik's bed, but I had a feeling that comment wouldn't endear me to her, despite her history of similar exploits.

"You know what, I don't care. Just get your ass in the changing room, right now. For crying out loud, did you sleep at all last night? You look like complete shit."

My best friend, ladies and gentleman. "I...slept. A bit."

"Yeah, and now I have to deal with the aftermath. Just look at you!" She waved a hand in front of my face. "Saggy eyes. Pale skin. Freshly-fucked hair."

I winced and lifted a hand to my head. Yup. A knotted mess. Awesome.

"Let's not even mention what you smell like. Lucky for you, I brought products for every scenario."

She shoved me through a magical door that led to a room full of a wide array of beauty products. Every warrior's worst nightmare. But I refused to make this more difficult for her. Lucy had gleefully accepted the request to mold me into a princess before the wedding, and I'd silently sworn I would sit back and submit. But, oh, the horror. I'd suffered countless nightmares about this moment. Our styles didn't mesh. Hell existed, and it consisted of lace, hairspray, and eye shadow.

"Sit," she barked, a tapered fingernail pointing at the chair.

*Here we go.*

I planted my butt in the chair and faced the mirror. A stranger stared back at me. I'd never had a one-night stand before, and I couldn't put my finger on which part I hated the most. That I'd loved every moment of it, or that it'd taken me this long to have one. Maybe I looked like shit, but inside, I felt alive. *Jerrik* had made me feel alive.

It had to be lingering hormones from the night before. Endorphins and whatnot. Nothing more. Quite unlikely that after one night, Jerrik himself made me feel this way. We'd only just met. And now, I'd never see him again.

"Sit still, would'ya?" Lucy hissed under her breath.

Right. Squirming wouldn't help the process.

"What's with you, anyway?" She tugged on the brush. I yelped, my hand flying to my tender scalp. "I can't believe you just vanished in the middle of your own party. Then ignored *all* my calls. Showed up late to your own wedding. This isn't like you! Last I saw, you were dancing with..." Her voice trailed off and her gaze snapped to mine in the mirror. "Oh, my God. You *didn't*!"

I fed her my most innocent stare. "Didn't, what?"

Her gaze roamed over my face, her brows narrowed. "No, you wouldn't."

I knew the direction her dirty little mind had taken, but I kept quiet. The last thing I needed were the gossip queens discussing my slight transgression. Lucy had my back, I knew that. But I *also* knew the moment she left this room, she'd tell *someone*. That someone would tell another someone. Before I knew it, *bam*, gossip. And while standing up at the altar saying *I do*, they'd be snickering into their palms saying *I bet she did*.

Thanks, but no thanks.

"Reagan!" she gasped. "Seriously? Tell me you didn't."

"Okay, I didn't. Can we finish this? Some of us have somewhere to be in..." I flicked a glance at my phone. "Forty-five minutes and counting."

"Reagan..."

"Later, Lucy, all right?" I snapped. "We have far more important things to worry about."

Like my upcoming nuptials. *Jesus*. The thought sent

a cold chill down my spine. But I refused to acknowledge my proverbial cold feet. Duty was duty. And this was mine.

Lucy returned to brushing my hair, her face stern as she tugged on my many knots. She clearly wanted to ask more questions, but we didn't have time for them. The next twenty minutes passed in awkward silence as she twisted my hair into a curled half up-do. She pinned the upper sections back and secured them with a pair of stylish pins. Then she moved onto my makeup. She rounded the chair and peered at my face, her mouth a grim line.

"Geez, Lucy. I'm not *that* hideous."

"Today, you are."

*Ouch*. Some friend.

"Now, hold still," she muttered.

She grabbed her makeup bag, dumped the contents, and attacked my face. By the time she'd finished, it felt as though she'd scrubbed my entire face raw. But when she stepped aside, I could see the effort had been worth it. My skin practically glowed, and her artistry had lent a mysterious edge to my dark eyes.

"Okay," she murmured, an eyeshadow brush dangling from her lips. "I think you're acceptable."

"Gee, thanks."

She shot me a half-grin, then turned. "But now comes the hard part."

I followed her gaze to the dress bag hanging against the back of the door. Next to it on the floor sat a duffel bag I'd stuffed full with a couple different thongs, my garter belt, and an assortment of bras. I'd chosen a strapless dress with a sweetheart cut, which hadn't left many choices for a bra. While we'd picked out a strapless one to match the gown, I hadn't liked the fit, constantly hiking it back up. A few nights ago—after many glasses of wine—Lucy and I had busted out our creative minds and put together a solution. A combination of self-adhesive gel inserts along with sports strapping tape, just in case. Anything to keep the girls locked in place, at least for a few hours. On the upside, my B-cup chest didn't require a whole lot of hold. At one point, I'd debated going without, but the material had chafed my nipples when I'd tried it on. So, sports tape and self-adhesive cups for the win.

I only hoped it worked. Today would be stressful enough without the added annoyance of fixing my boobs every few minutes.

"Ready?" she asked me.

I inhaled and nodded. Now or never.

Lucy strode to the bag and unzipped it, careful not to snag the material. "I have to say, it's beautiful."

I eyed the pearly white gown. I would have preferred a simple white dress in city hall, but my father had insisted on a massive celebration. *If we're going to do this, we're going to do it with style,* he'd said. I'd lacked the courage to tell him no. This would be his one and only chance to walk his daughter down the aisle. Last I'd heard, my father had invited the entire pack, all seven thousand three hundred of us, plus an additional three thousand from the one European pack he'd kept as an ally. Thankfully, only four hundred and twenty-eight had accepted. Those who personally knew me and my father, or Benjamin and his. All about politics, my father had assured me. Invite them so they can't complain.

Still, four hundred and twenty-eight people. I hoped the gardens in the back were large enough. My father had assured me they were.

"All right, let's do this," Lucy said. "Twenty-three minutes until show-time."

I stripped off my clothes from last night and slid on the undergarments, complete with dagger strapped to my thigh. Old habits. After applying the self-adhesive cups, we opted for a few extra strips of tape as a precaution. Then Lucy removed the dress from the hanger and held it out to me. I stepped into it, wiggled it up over my slender hips, and held it to my chest. Lucy toed around me, careful of the train, and quickly fastened the numerous buttons in the back.

"There!" she announced. "Twelve minutes to spare."

*Twelve minutes.* I closed my eyes and inhaled a long breath. *Holy shit.* In twelve minutes, my father would knock on the door and escort me out into the garden where *four hundred and twenty-eight* people waited. Not including the groom and his father.

"Lucy..." I whispered. "I...need... I need a moment."

She shot me a worried glance. "You okay?"

I shook my head and staggered to the chair. I eased down onto it and leaned as far forward as the rigid corset would allow.

"You need some water," she announced.

I nodded eagerly. Water sounded amazing. And air. My lungs definitely needed some air.

"Is the dress too tight?" she asked, studying the lines.

I shook my head. Uncomfortable, yes, but not too tight. "Just need a minute. Please."

"I'll go get some water. You'll feel better."

Doubtful. But I needed her gone so I could think. Needed a moment to pull myself together. My father, Benjamin, *everyone* was waiting on me. I imagined them all standing out in the gardens, chattering amongst themselves, shaking hands, congratulating my future husband...

*Husband.*

The room started to swim, and gray dots crept in on my vision. A panic attack. Yup, just what I needed right now. I couldn't do this. *Sweet Jesus*, I couldn't. I shook my head and launched to my feet. If I made a break for it now...

*No!*

I forced myself still and closed my eyes. *Three deep breaths. In and out. You can do this.* I nodded, listening to the sound of my own voice to center my thoughts.

*Inhale.*

My chest rose as I filled my lungs.

*Exhale.*

And deflated when I emptied them.

I repeated that process three more times until my heart and pulse had returned to normal. The little spots had vanished, but my body still felt weak, my knees trembling as they fought to hold me up.

"One step at a time," I whispered to myself. "Don't think about the end goal. Right now, just focus on the door."

My dad would knock, and he'd take my arm. Baby steps.

Sure enough, a knock resounded through my room. My head snapped up, and there went my heart again. Beating an erratic tattoo. Lucy hadn't even returned with my water yet. But it didn't matter. The moment had come.

*I can do this. I can. One step. Then another. Just open the door.*

With one last steadying breath, I opened the door and froze.

*Jerrik.*

*WHAT THE FUCKEDY FUCK?*

This had to be a full on hallucination, right? A wonderful delirium inspired by my panic attack? I honestly couldn't imagine any other reason why Jerrik would be standing in front of me. And looking as mouth-wateringly delicious as ever in that same leather jacket.

He stood in the doorway, his hands clutching at the frame and his head hanging low. But when he glanced up, his mouth fell slack and his cold eyes thawed. He straightened, his jaw clenching as he drank in the sight of me. "Shit, Reagan. Wow. I can't even... You look...incredible."

Considering the circumstances, I shouldn't have smiled. But tell that to my heart. For some reason, his opinion mattered, and I loved rendering him speechless.

I glanced past him and spotted Lucy off in the

distance, her back to me as she filled up a bottle of water at the fountain. She hadn't seen him yet, thank goodness. I didn't want to imagine her reaction.

I turned back to Jerrik. "Thanks, but what are you doing here?"

He gave a slow blink, then stepped into the room and shut the door behind him. He surveyed our surroundings, grabbed the chair, and tucked it under the doorknob, locking us in. Then he strode to the far window and peeked outside, his fingers turning the notch.

"Jerrik?"

"Get dressed," he said suddenly.

"Uh...I am dressed."

"No, I mean..." He turned back and waved at my pile of discarded clothing. "You need to change. Out of the dress."

I lifted a brow. I'd played out this day many times in my head throughout the past couple of months, but I'd never once envisioned this. Not even my imagination could have conceived my one-night stand tracking me down the day of my wedding. I couldn't imagine this ending well, considering my father was due in a minute or two. He wouldn't take kindly to any of this.

"In case you've forgotten, I'm getting married today," I whispered, afraid someone would overhear in the hallway. "So, I don't know what's going on with you, but this really isn't the right time."

"You aren't getting married today," he said matter-of-factly.

Laughter rushed past my lips before I could stop myself. "Sure, okay."

"I'm serious, Reagan. You need to get dressed, now. We need to go."

"Jerrik—"

"How long have you been here?" he interrupted.

"What?"

He dragged a hand through his hair and blew out a heavy breath. "How *long*, Reagan? When did you wake up? When did you get here?"

His frantic voice plucked at my nerves. I placed a hand to my stomach and glanced back at the door. "Just shy of an hour ago, why?"

"Shit. He knows, then."

I shook my head. "Who knows what? What are you talking about?"

"I don't have the time to explain this right now."

"Then *make* the time," I growled. "You can't barge in here and demand I leave my wedding with you without any explanation."

"I need you to trust me."

My brows shot up. "Just like that?"

"You trusted me last night," he pointed out. "Several times."

Blood rushed to my cheeks and I ducked my head. "That was different."

"No, it wasn't." He started toward me, his every step riddled with a strength I'd seen in few others. "You trusted me last night. You went home with me, because something about me calls to you. I'd like to believe that if you had a choice you wouldn't be here right now."

*Oh, my God.* Was that what this was about? Jealousy? Stupid male werewolf drama? "It was one night."

"It was more than that, and you know it. Whether you want to admit it or not. But that's not why I'm here." He took another step, his overwhelming presence forcing me backward.

I lifted my chin and met his glacial stare. "Then tell me why you're here."

The doorknob jiggled behind me. Both Jerrik and I shot it a glance, but before I could move, he reached out and snatched my hand.

"Reagan?" Lucy called out in the hallway.

"Don't," he growled under his breath. "Don't call back to her."

"Reagan? Is someone in there with you?"

I shot Jerrik a wry glance. Werewolves—of course she'd heard his voice.

He stared down at me, a golden light slowly spreading through his eyes as his wolf came out to play. Seemed I had two options. Send Lucy away and hear him out, or call to her for help. I didn't know Jerrik well, but I couldn't deny the chemistry between us. His fingers curled gently around my wrist. I could break his hold at any time. I just didn't want to. And the way he looked at me, I couldn't explain it, but I *did* trust him.

*Call me a fool.*

He lifted his other hand and cupped my face, his thumb stroking my cheek. I pressed into his hand with a soft sigh.

*Trust me*, he mouthed.

I had a feeling I'd regret this, but I nodded. Relief loosened his shoulders and he gestured toward the door.

"I'm fine, Lucy, thanks. Just give me a few more minutes."

"Are you kidding me?" she yelled through the door. "You know we're starting soon, right?"

"Reagan?" my father's voice rose in the hallway. "Lucy, what's wrong?"

"She won't open the door."

"Reagan, honey, is everything okay?"

Of course my father had chosen *this* exact moment to appear. "I'm fine, Dad. I just need a few minutes, okay?"

"Sure, honey. Take all the time you need. We'll wait out here."

Lucy groaned, but her hand fell away from the door. "The things I do for you, woman."

I listened with half an ear as both Lucy and my father retreated down the hallway. As far as they knew, there wasn't any reason to hover.

I turned back to Jerrik. "You have sixty seconds, and then I'm opening that door."

"Easy." He locked eyes with me, his palm still firm against my cheek. "Your fiancé wants you dead."

A few seconds passed in silence while I waited for the other shoe to drop. Laughter, a wink, a hearty *gotcha* before he turned and strode out the door. Nadda. He held still, watching as I digested the strangest thing I'd ever heard someone say.

"Ha, ha, very funny. Can you be serious, please?"

"I am being serious, Reagan. Your fiancé hired an assassin to kill you."

"Right, okay. And why the hell would he do that? Not to toot my own horn, but marrying me is kind of a big deal. Heir to the North American pack, and all that. Why would *anyone* want to assassinate me?"

"Because your death would weaken your father."

*My father?* How the hell would killing me weaken my father? I shook my head and took a step back. "This doesn't make any sense."

"Think, Reagan. How would your father react to your death?"

"He'd be..." I paused, then blew out a heavy breath as understanding dawned. "He'd be heartbroken."

"Exactly. And a heartbroken alpha is a vulnerable alpha. You mean everything to your father, everyone knows that. He adores you. Your death would weaken your father emotionally and give Benjamin a chance to challenge. If he won, he'd take over the entire pack."

"But *why* would he go through all that? He's marrying me, which practically *gives* him the pack. What would killing me accomplish?"

Jerrik's expression softened. "Your father stipulated in the agreement that Benjamin, his father, and their people could move west and join your pack, but that's it. Your father told them they would have no hand in running the pack, even their own people. They would remain alphas, but all pack matters would fall to Gabriel. And in the event of your father's death, the pack would go to you. They've been given no rights beyond that."

I lifted a hand to my brow and pinched the bridge of my nose. My father had never mentioned any of this. Why would he have kept it from me?

"Do you understand now, dove?" Jerrik took my hand in his and used his other to guide my chin up. "Benjamin thought marrying you meant he'd eventually run the pack. He wants *more* than marrying you. And this arrangement isn't ideal for him. So, he's changing the game. With you out of the picture, he weakens your father and the pack in one blow. And if he challenges your father—who would have to accept—and wins... No alpha, no heir, no one left to stand in his way."

"He becomes the alpha of the entire pack."

"Along with his own when his father passes. He'd control all of North America and Europe."

Pack domination.

I staggered backward and leaned against the counter, my fingers gripping the smooth edge of the workspace. I didn't want to believe what I'd heard. Benjamin wouldn't... Wouldn't what? Plot my father's and my demise? I didn't know that. I didn't know a thing about him other than what I'd heard from my father. And he likely didn't know much more. My father and Christian had been friends since before colonization, but that meant very little if they hadn't seen one another in two or three centuries. And maybe Christian had no part in this.

"How do you know all this?" I whispered, my fingers touching my lips.

"I hear things." When I lifted a brow, he blew out a harsh breath. "Does it really matter right now?"

No, it didn't. Not at the moment. "I need to talk to my father. I need to tell him about this."

Jerrik stepped in front of me before I could move. "You can't."

"Excuse me?" I tipped my head back and eyed him. "What do you mean I can't? My father *needs* to know."

"And he will, when we have proof."

My jaw slackened. Who gave a damn about proof? My father would take my word over Benjamin and Christian's any day of the week.

I skirted around Jerrik and started for the door. "Sorry, but I'm telling him."

Jerrik cursed under his breath, then pulled me back just as my fingers grazed the doorknob. "Reagan, we don't have time for this."

"What are you talking about? Of course we do. My father is right outside the door, and—"

"And if he sees me, he'll attack before either of us can utter a word."

"You're being ridiculous. My father doesn't even know you. So let me talk to him—"

Jerrik's long fingers tightened around my arm as he drew me back to the center of the room. He dipped his head and looked me in the eyes. "Believe me. The second Gabriel spots me, it'll be a fight, and I really don't want to kill your father."

I laughed. I couldn't help it. Jerrik was strong, sure. But my father was the pack alpha. He hadn't risen to that status through speeches and pretty promises. There was no democracy in the pack. Only the strongest held it. Which was why Benjamin meant to resort to cheating. In a fair fight, I doubted any werewolf alive could best my father.

With an amused smile, I reached up and cupped Jerrik's face. "You don't have to worry about fighting Gabriel. I won't let it come to that."

A harsh sound rushed past Jerrik's lips. "That's not...

Listen to me, Reagan. Gabriel and I have a rocky history. Opening that door right now won't end well for either of us."

"What do you mean, a rocky history?"

Jerrik's eyes closed, and for a brief moment, I felt bereft. When they flashed open, they were aglow with his wolf, golden streaks sparking through his beautiful eyes. "Gabriel and I first met a few centuries ago when he demanded I submit to him and I refused."

I blinked. "You refused? But that's..."

"A direct challenge," Jerrik whispered. "He told me that if I refused to fall in and obey, he'd kill me."

I nodded. Standard procedure for misbehaving wolves.

"Notice how I'm still alive?" he murmured.

"Reagan?" my father's voice rose in the hallway, distracting me from any further questions. "Sweetheart, we really do need to get started."

Jerrik leaned in close and barely breathed the words into my ear. "And we need to go, now. I swear, I'll tell you the rest later."

"You're asking me to walk out on everyone," I whispered. "My father, Lucy, my pack..."

He nodded.

"Reagan?" my father called out. "Honey?"

Jerrik turned and led me toward the window. "You can call your father later and explain the situation."

*So much for changing out of my dress.* I chewed the inside of my bottom lip and glanced back at the door. The two people I loved the most stood on the other side, waiting to walk me down the aisle. But if Jerrik was telling the truth, I couldn't marry Benjamin.

"Reagan," he whispered so quietly I could barely hear him.

I shot him a glance, and with a heavy heart, nodded. It wouldn't be long now before my father broke down the door in search of me. If Jerrik spoke the truth, he needed to be as far away as possible when that moment came. And I had too many questions to let him run off on his own.

His fingers squeezed mine once before he popped open the window and hopped out. He turned back and offered me a hand, helping to untangle my dress when it snagged. But once I stood on the other side, I felt a freedom I'd never felt before. No impending wedding, no murderous fiancé breathing down my neck. Nothing but the wind and the scent of pine as we tore through the nearby forest, hand in hand.

"Well now. Aren't you two simply the cutest!"

I lifted my head, my attention landing on the woman standing behind the counter. Clad in a bright blue t-shirt trimmed with yellow, she stood next to a register with a beaming grin and a nametag that read *Stacy*. Surely she had to be talking about someone else. But her gaze locked with mine, reaffirming that she'd spoken to me.

Jerrik stood next to me, his hands tucked in his pockets. With a half-cocked grin, he shot me a wink, then rocked back onto his heels and stared up at the menu.

"Did you just get married?" Stacy asked in a squeaky voice.

Did we just…? I shot her a glance, wondering if I was allowed to respond sarcastically to such a stupid question. Jerrik wore faded jeans and his brown leather jacket. What groom wore that for his wedding? But my mother ways been a firm believer in manners. Amalie Saint-George would have slapped the smirk off my face had she been alive to see it.

"Uh, no," I said as I stepped up to the counter. "He's my..." Shit, I had no idea how to explain this.

"Chauffeur," Jerrik suggested. "Gotta get this beautiful blushing bride to the church, don't I? But you know how it is." He leaned against the counter and tossed Stacy a saucy wink. "When the bride says she's hungry, it's best to pull over and get her something to eat, you know? Especially on her wedding day. Security policy, so she doesn't eat me."

Stacy laughed, color flushing her cheeks as Jerrik held her attention.

Oddly enough, his story held some truth. After ducking through the woods, I'd suggested we stop for a bite to eat. My last meal had been last night's cock-cake, which definitely wasn't cutting it after our rather amorous evening, and I couldn't think on an empty stomach.

"What can I get for you, then?" Stacy's gaze cut to mine for a brief second before darting back to Jerrik.

I almost laughed. Here I stood, decked out in a beautiful gown and my face polished until it shone, but her eyes were all for him. I wasn't complaining, though. He was purposely keeping the attention off me. The last thing we needed was for someone to recognize me.

"Why don't you surprise me, sweetheart," Jerrik said in a seductive voice.

Stacy simpered and dropped her attention to the register. She punched in a few codes and rang up two different meals. Extra fries and ice cream on the side, of course.

My mouth quirked, though I felt bad for the human... a little. The way she preened for him—tucking her hair back and moistening her lips. As though she believed she stood a chance in hell with someone like him.

He dropped a few bills onto the counter and took the tray from her with a flirtatious grin. I grabbed a table in the back and gestured toward it. When we sat, the grin slipped from his face and he cast another vigilant glance around the restaurant. For a Saturday, it seemed quiet. A few elderly couples sat in their booths, nursing their cups of coffee while talking about the good ol' days. No one paid us any mind.

"We need to find you some clothes," Jerrik commented as he surveyed the restaurant.

"Hmm." I grabbed a fry and popped it into my mouth. "And here I thought you liked my dress."

His stare cut to me, gold rolling over his eyes. "Darlin', I would tear that thing off you in a heartbeat if I could. But it might scandalize the civilians."

"And poor Stacy," I teased.

He groaned and leaned back in his seat, one arm slung over the booth. I couldn't help but appreciate the view. His leather jacket slipped open, revealing a snug black t-shirt, clearly the brother to the white one he'd worn last night. But it didn't matter what he wore, I knew what lay beneath. The peaks and valleys, the hard definition of his lickable abs, the swell of his arms as he moved above me...oh yes, I knew them well.

On the upside, at least I hadn't married Benjamin

And knowing what I now knew, I no longer felt the slightest bit of guilt for sleeping with Jerrik.

I lifted what looked like a chicken wrap and downed it in three bites.

Jerrik watched in amusement, his brow lifted. "Guess you weren't lying when you said you were hungry."

"Starved, actually," I said after swallowing. "Chocolate cake doesn't go very far."

Desire lit up his eyes. "Did for me."

The strangeness of this moment wasn't lost on me. This morning before leaving Jerrik's house, I might have given anything for this moment. But I'd never imagined it while on the lam from my own fiancé.

"All right," I murmured. "Out with it."

The gold dimmed in his eyes. "Out with what?"

"Everything."

"Reagan, I've told you everything."

No, he hadn't. Not by a long shot. I still had so many questions.

He pulled in his arm and leaned against the table. "Is this really the right time?"

I gestured toward our surroundings. "As good a time as any, wouldn't you agree? No one's recognized us. Stacy is too busy imagining her own wedding, so long as you're the groom—"

He grimaced.

"—and I'm fed. Which means, I'm ready for the full truth."

"Reagan."

I leaned closer and dropped my voice. "Look. I know you didn't tell me everything. I'm not some wilting little flower that you need to protect. So, how about you drop the over-protective act and speak to me, alpha to alpha."

He sighed, then sat back and raked a hand through his hair. After a moment's silence, he met my gaze. "It's not an act, you know."

"What's not?"

He waved between us. "This. And I know you're not a wilting flower. Hell, Gabriel raised you. From what I know about him, I'm guessing you could drop everyone in this restaurant without breaking a sweat, me being the exception."

"I don't know, I dropped you hard last night," I said, hoping to inspire a little levity. He wasn't the only one who could tease.

Astonishment widened his eyes.

I grinned, then reached for another fry. "So, if this isn't an act, then what is it?"

"It's who I am," he said. "I'm old. And very much set in my ways. And—"

"How old?"

He froze, his tirade dying on his lips.

"Don't tell me you can't even answer that simple question."

"It's not so simple," he countered.

"Actually, it is. See, if someone asked me how old I was, I would respond with a hundred and two." I gestured toward him. "Your turn."

"I don't remember the exact year," he commented.

I raised my brows. Who didn't remember the year they were born?

"But if I had to guess, I'd say a thousand and some change."

This time, I froze, a fry dangling halfway to my mouth. A *thousand* and some change? I stared at him, too stunned to formulate a response. And here I'd thought my father was old.

My father had insisted my mother homeschool me, so I knew all about our history. I knew that the pack had emigrated from Europe in the early fifteen hundreds. If what Jerrik had said was true, he would have already been old at that point.

"Wow," I whispered, completely unsure of what else to say. His earlier words about my father echoed in my head. It all made sense now. "You said you and Gabriel had met before. That he challenged you."

"And lost," Jerrik filled in. "But that was a long, long time ago. After he led the pack here."

I held up a hand. "Wait, after he *led* the pack here? You're saying *you* were here first?"

His head bobbed.

*Holy shit. Holy fucking shit.* "How long have you been in America?"

"A long time," was all he said.

"Yeah, but how long? When did you first come here?"

His jaw tightened and he turned away as a darkness rippled across his face. "Shouldn't we focus on the problem at hand?"

Right. The problem at hand. My fiancé wanted me dead. A pretty big problem. But damn. Hard to focus on something like that when the man sitting before me was literally a part of North American history. Had lived and breathed it. There were so many questions I wanted to ask, but something else came to mind. Pieces of stories my father had told me throughout my life.

I cocked my head as I recalled them. I'd never given the stories much consideration—I'd always believed they were nothing more than tales my father had concocted to amuse his daughter. But he'd always warned me about the *shadow wolf*, as he'd called him. The wolf older than time itself, who had refused to join the pack, who had chosen isolation...

Who hated his own kind and killed them for profit. An assassin.

"Oh, my God," I whispered, my lungs deflating. "You're *him*."

Gabriel had never spoken that wolf's name before. But I knew it now, didn't I? Jerrik, the shadow wolf. What did I know about him? So much. *Too* much.

"What? Who?"

"Oh, my God," I repeated. I ran a hand down my face, my heart squeezing into a painful knot. Maybe I was naïve, and a bit of a fool, but I could put the puzzle together once I had all the pieces. And every last one of them sat before me. Even the illusive center.

"Reagan." Jerrik reached across the table.

I wrenched my hand back before we made contact. "Don't touch me," I hissed.

He blinked, startled by my sudden reaction.

My thoughts strayed to the dagger strapped to my thigh. If not for this *stupid* dress, I might have been able to reach it. But that would require fishing beneath yards of fabric. Not exactly discreet.

"Listen to me—"

My laughter cut him off. "Listen to *you*? An assassin?"

He froze, then released a long breath as he leaned back in the booth.

*Yeah, that's right. I figured you out.* "I don't know what kind of sick game you're playing, but I'm done. Hear me?" I cursed under my breath. "How much of this was even true? Was this all part of your plan? Get me alone, seduce me, tell me my fiancé wanted me dead... Then what? What's your end goal here? God, I'm so *stupid!*"

"Reagan..."

Bitter laughter slipped past my lips. "My father told me about you. Told me about the Viking wolf turned mercenary. The assassin. So, that's all this was to you? A game?"

"Listen to me. I'm not playing around here. Benjamin wants you dead."

"Yeah, and he paid you to do it."

Jerrik fell silent, his mouth parted in shock, as though he hadn't expected me to put it all together. A math expert I was not, but I knew two plus two equaled four.

"That's why you were at the club last night. Scoping me out? Planning your move? Then you thought, hey, maybe I can score a quick piece of ass before killing her?"

"That's not—"

"Save it," I growled. I scoffed under my breath and surged to my feet, which took effort thanks to the friggin' dress. "I can't believe I fell for it. You know, last night I wondered why you'd be interested in me. If it was some bet. But I'd never imagined this."

He stood and shot a glance around the restaurant. "If I wanted you dead, don't you think I would have done it by now? Yes, Benjamin hired me, but I decided not to follow through with the contract."

"Oh, how magnanimous of you," I snapped.

"Would you stop? Listen to me. You're in danger, I can protect you—"

"That's not the way I see it. I'm heading back to the church to find my father, like I initially wanted."

Jerrik stepped in front of me. "It isn't safe out there, and you aren't armed right now."

So angry with myself, with Jerrik, and with the world, I scooped up the hem of my dress, lifted it up to my hips and extracted the blade. Before my skirt even hit the ground, I had it pressed against his side, hidden from everyone else's sights.

This close to him, my body hummed with awareness. I shoved those feelings down deep and met his stare. "I don't go *anywhere* unarmed. Trust me when I say this is silver and will drop you."

A hint of a smile curved the corners of his mouth. "A woman after my own heart. Damn, I would have loved to have met you when I was human. You would have made a wonderful Viking."

His words struck a chord within me. The majority of us were born werewolves. Only a few were ever bitten and changed. Jerrik's words...had someone bitten him? But before my curiosity distracted me, I shoved that thought aside and pushed the tip of my blade into his jacket, cutting through the beautiful material. "I'm going to walk out the door, and you're going to let me."

Jerrik lifted a dark brow. "Am I now? You know who I am, so why not just kill me?"

"Goodbye, Jerrik."

I removed the knife from his side and hid it in the folds of my dress. Wouldn't do to upset the locals. I braved a step back, unsurprised when Jerrik followed me. "I'm leaving."

"What a coincidence, so am I."

"Without you," I said through gritted teeth.

He clasped his hands together behind his back and matched my second step. "Sorry. But no."

Annoyance knotted my brow. He moved with a fluidness that contradicted his watchful eye. I cursed under my breath and repositioned my grip around the dagger's hilt. I really didn't want to attack him in public, but if he forced my hand, at least I had good reason.

"What's the matter?" he taunted. "Thought you were ready to drop me?"

He knew I wouldn't unless he pushed me too far. Generally speaking, stabbing someone in front of witnesses never ended well.

"Stop following me."

"Can't," he said with a shrug. "I promised myself I'd protect you."

"I don't *need* your protection," I snapped. "I'm perfectly capable of taking care of myself."

I backed into the door, my heel catching on the edge of my dress, and stumbled. First chance I got, I'd burn this blasted thing. I never wanted to lay eyes on it again.

"Watch your step," Jerrik called to me, his blue eyes shining with amusement.

*Bastard.* Of course he'd find this funny.

"Might help if you look where you're going."

I staggered out into the parking lot. Things were about to become complicated. I couldn't keep watching him while walking, but I didn't want him following me either. And much like the idiot I'd already proven myself to be, I'd left my cellphone and wallet back at the church.

*See, that's what happens when you follow a stranger out a window...*

"Reagan, this is silly," Jerrik commented once we stood in the parking lot. "Obviously, I'm not going to hurt you. But you're going to get hurt if you keep walking around like this. People can see us, you know. And you're not exactly blending in."

"So, leave," I snapped. "Let me go back to the church."

"I thought you were this big bad warrior?" He canted his head, a challenge gleaming in his eyes. "You want me to leave? Make me."

I didn't quite know how to respond to that. A part of me *wanted* to attack, but the disadvantages were overwhelming. My one blade against whatever he was packing. Not to mention his pants versus my dress. He had the upper hand in every way. And he knew it.

"How do I know you're even telling the truth?" I finally asked. "You're asking me to take the word of an assassin. Someone who took a contract to *kill* me!"

"And then didn't! Doesn't that win me any brownie points?"

I laughed. "You're kidding, right? You're asking me to *thank* you for not killing me?"

Alarm flashed in Jerrik's eyes. But before I could respond, a firm hand gripped my throat and wrenched me back.

"If you won't thank him," a gruff voice rasped in my ear. "I will."

Jerrik stilled, cold determination settling over his face as he evaluated the situation. Nothing to evaluate, as far as I was concerned. Whoever stood behind me would die, as simple as that. I didn't take kindly to the gun jabbed into my back, or to the fingers pinching my throat, ready to rip it out without a moment's notice.

"Let me guess," I commented in a bored voice. "Another one of Benjamin's assassins?"

The hand at my throat gave me a hard shake. "Shut up."

*Yeah. Because that always works.* I sighed and leaned into him, forcing him to counter a bit of my weight.

"You know, this is a *really* bad idea. Not only do you have to take me out, but then you'll have to take him out, too." I jerked my chin toward Jerrik. "If you kill me, what's to stop him from killing *you* and collecting the reward himself?"

Fury lit up Jerrik's eyes in a startling gold that sucked me in. An interesting reaction considering he'd intended to kill me himself. Angry that someone else got the upper hand? His every muscle went rigid, his hands clenched at his sides. Needless to say, whoever stood at my back had pissed off the shadow wolf. Not to mention me.

Not a great start to his day.

"I have the gun," my captor growled in my ear.

I almost laughed. Like a gun would make a difference. Sure, it'd take me out if he'd loaded it with silver bullets. But a wolf like Jerrik? The jackass at my back wouldn't even get the second shot off before Jerrik ripped out his heart. Or, so I assumed. But it seemed a safe bet when dealing with someone like the shadow wolf. I'd heard the stories about him throughout my life. At the time, I'd thought them exaggerated. Guess I was about to find out.

I caught Jerrik's eyes again and watched as they flicked down to my hand. I gave a subtle nod. He didn't need to remind me of the blade clutched between my fingers.

"What's your name?" I asked.

"Shut up," he snapped, giving me another shake. I swear, this time I heard my eyeballs rattle around in my head.

"Come on, it's not that hard. All I want to know is the name of the man who wants to kill me. Is that so much to ask?"

He hesitated, his fingers flexing against my throat, as though contemplating whether or not to rip it out.

"David," he finally muttered.

David, the Assassin. Huh—not quite what I'd expected.

"Well, David. Let me tell you how this is going to go down. If you shoot me, you'll have to drop me and lift your gun. But Jerrik is fast. Faster than you I bet."

Jerrik's eyes went cold, and the corners of his mouth lifted.

"So, shoot me if you want. I'm just saying maybe there's a better solution here."

"Solution? You're worth half a mill dead."

I whistled. Benjamin had definitely gone all out.

"No way of talking you out of this, then?" I asked.

"Not unless you want to offer me a million."

Wow. A million. "Good to know how much my life is worth. Makes me feel all warm inside."

"Shut the fuck up!" David shouted.

"Did you even take into consideration how badly you've screwed up?" I asked. "We're in a parking lot. In the middle of the day. Someone has probably already called the cops."

His body tensed behind me.

"Jesus. You didn't even think this through, did you, David? You just saw the dollar signs."

"I'm getting tired of your mouth."

Yeah, me and him both.

"Run now, while you can," I said, the last bit of advice I had to offer.

Jerrik tensed, ready to rush forward. But to what end?

To protect me, or to stop someone else from killing me? He'd claimed he wanted to help, but right now, I didn't know what to believe, surrounded by assassins as it was. The only one I could trust here was me.

And when David shifted his weight, I took control of the situation.

With a deep breath, I slammed the back of my head into his nose. It shattered with a sickening crunch. David shouted and staggered backward, releasing me from his hold. I spun around and knocked his gun to the ground with a quick blow. I followed through with another jab to his gut before darting behind him. I fisted a hand in his hair, wrenched his head back, and pressed my blade against his exposed throat.

My gaze darted to Jerrik. He stared at me, his lips parted with surprise. Shocked, perhaps, that I'd handled the problem without his help? It angered me when people assumed I couldn't take care of myself. Or suggested I needed others to handle things for me. For nearly a century, I'd trained under Gabriel's tutelage. Though my mother had disagreed with my upbringing, Gabriel had deemed it crucial. I remembered their legendary fights, where she'd insisted I be raised like a lady. Even now, I recalled Gabriel's biting response, that as his heir I needed to be more than that. That he refused to raise me in my mother's image—the doting princess who wouldn't lift a hand to save her own life. That same day, he'd started training me with swords.

I'd been nine.

Every time my mother complained, he'd added a new regimen, as though to prove to her that I could handle it.

Hand-to-hand combat, swordplay, guns, spears...he'd made me an expert in every form of weaponry.

And it'd paid off.

"Half a million wasn't nearly enough," I whispered in David's ear.

Poor guy trembled against me, his Adam's apple bobbing against the silver blade.

Sirens wailed in the background. I cursed inwardly and debated our options. One sharp pull and David would drop dead on the pavement. But then I still had Jerrik to handle. And I didn't want to involve the cops. Werewolf business wasn't meant for human ears.

"Reagan, we need to go," Jerrik commented.

"I'm not going anywhere with you."

"You can trust me," he urged. "I swear to you, I have no desire to kill you."

"Not even for half a million?"

Jerrik's mouth split into a wide grin. "Chump change for me, dove."

I didn't have time to argue. We were seconds away from the police arresting us, and every bone in my body wanted to avoid that. I'd suffered enough limelight in my life without adding more fuel to the fire. The reporters would leap on this story if I gave them the chance. Reagan Compton, arrested after bailing on her wedding.

The impending headlines were enough to convince me.

"You swear that you have no intentions of collecting on Benjamin's contract?" I demanded.

"If I intended to kill you, I would have last night. You know that."

My fingers tightened in David's hair. That just left him. I couldn't simply release him. He'd think me weak and try again. But killing him wasn't an option, either.

I lowered my blade from David's neck and released his hair. But before he could straighten, I slammed the blade home and drove it through his side. He screamed and dropped to his knees, clutching at the hilt as blood spilled over his hands.

"Oh, knock it off," I grumped. "I missed anything vital, you'll be fine."

I reached down and knocked his hands out of the way. My fingers closed around the hilt and I wrenched the blade free. Wouldn't do to lose a perfectly good weapon, especially with a contract on my life. David cried out and toppled to the ground, his fingers stained red.

"Reagan," Jerrik said. He reached out and grabbed my arm. "We need to go, now."

I nodded. After a final glance in David's direction, I turned and followed Jerrik. With luck, David would pick himself up and be gone before the cops arrived. We werewolves were tough sons of bitches.

---

I FOLLOWED Jerrik into his house, and shot him a glance when the door slammed shut behind me. The gold sheen to his eyes hadn't ebbed in the time it'd taken us to return here. In fact, with every blink, they seemed to burn a little bit brighter. I hadn't a clue what thoughts were traipsing through his head, but seemed safe to say he was pissed.

And I had a pretty good idea as to why.

Maybe stabbing David had taken things a step too far, but it'd driven my point home. One David would remember until his dying day—which was a hell of a lot closer after pulling that stunt. David was a walking dead man. Once my father caught word of all this, he'd send out a search party. Might have been best if I *had* killed him.

Jerrik stormed through his house, his heavy boots echoing on the hardwood flooring. The pungent stench of rage followed in his wake, perfuming the air. I stood in the entryway, not entirely sure how to proceed. Last night, we'd stumbled into his bedroom, a tangle of limbs the second we'd toppled onto his mattress. Today, not so much. He wouldn't even look at me.

Standing here wouldn't accomplish anything. So, I kicked off my heels and tiptoed into his bedroom. I'd left my bag of clothes at the church, but I refused to wear this stupid dress a moment longer. I wanted out of the confining bodice, and I never wanted to lay eyes on a white gown again. Unfortunately, no matter how I twisted or turned, I couldn't reach the damn buttons.

Anger welled within me. I closed my eyes and focused on breathing. With every exhalation, I tried to expel my frustration. *Focus on the positives. You're alive. You're not married to that rat-bastard. And you got to stab someone.* All wins in my book.

"What are you doing?" Jerrik demanded in a dark voice, ruining my Zen moment.

With my eyes still closed, I held up a hand. "I need out of this dress, but I can't reach the buttons. So, I'm meditating for a moment instead of punching a hole in the wall."

I listened to the sound of his boots thumping against the floor as he closed the distance between us. His fingers brushed the hair away from the nape of my neck, and my skin puckered. Even after everything today, his damn touch electrified me. If that didn't make me hate myself a little more, I didn't know what would.

He pushed my hair aside, his breath fanning the back of my neck. "That's a lot of buttons."

"All the better to piss me off," I grumbled.

"Do you care about the dress?"

"Just get it off me," I snapped.

I heard the distinctive sound of a pocket knife snapping open. "Hold still."

The blade cleaved down the back of my dress, quickly loosening the bodice to the point where I could breathe again. Just like that, my anger and frustration evaporated. With a relieved sigh, I held the dress close to my chest and turned.

Jerrik's eyes blazed even as they raked me over. Clearly he was still pissed.

"Look, I'm sorry I stabbed him," I said.

He blinked, the light dimming. "What?"

"You're mad. I probably shouldn't have stabbed David. But I couldn't kill him in public like that, and I couldn't just let him go. In my defense, the bastard had it coming."

"You think I'm mad that you stabbed him?"

I lifted a brow. "Aren't you?"

Jerrik sighed and lifted a hand to his brow, pinching the bridge of his nose. He muttered something incomprehensible under his breath. When his eyes opened, the gold had faded, leaving behind his beautiful baby blues. "Reagan, I don't give a shit that you stabbed him."

"Then what's with the stomping around and growly voice?" Granted, I didn't know him well, but to me, those rang close to rage.

"I'm pissed that the fucker found you. That he held a gun to you. That he laid his fucking hands on you."

All right. Didn't expect that answer.

"I would kill him right now if I could. Rip his damn head off and deliver it to Benjamin myself."

My mouth twitched, but I bit back my laughter.

"What?" he snapped. "What's so damn funny?"

"You really don't want me dead," I said.

"And that's amusing to you?"

"Well, you are the shadow wolf. Last I heard, you didn't really care about other werewolves. Just money. Benjamin dangled half a million in front of your face, and you walked away from it. Yeah, I find that funny."

"Happy to oblige," he growled.

"Oh, come on. You have to see the humor in this, too. You're probably the scariest werewolf in the world, and here you are playing protector."

He blinked at me. "What the hell did your father tell you?"

"Nothing I'm sure you haven't heard. Deadliest

assassin in North America. Takes pride in his job. Loves killing. Blah, blah, blah."

Jerrik chuckled under his breath and shook his head. "Only you would make light of such a thing. Yes, I chose isolation. Because I was ancient before your father and his pack even crossed onto this land. When he approached me, he didn't ask if I wanted to join. He demanded that I submit and obey."

Yeah, that sounded like Gabriel. The man wasn't known for his manners.

"When I *disobeyed*, he thought he'd forcibly show me what it meant to obey an alpha. He didn't stop and think. He just attacked. And I put him down."

"Why didn't you kill him?"

Jerrik shrugged. "Killing him meant I'd have to become the alpha. Fate worse than death if you ask me. I've been alone since before the dark ages. I prefer my solitude." His face hardened. "And I never want to be responsible for someone else's life again."

"But you want to help me?"

"That's different. *You're* different."

I lifted a brow. "How so?"

"It doesn't matter. You're safe here, that's what matters. No one knows of this place. I've kept it a secret for the past ten years or so."

I glanced around his room and nodded. A safe house of sorts. "It's a nice place."

"Thanks."

I actually liked his style. The soft yellow lighting, the dark dresser and bed frame that offset the creamy-colored walls. They lent the room a homey feel that my place lacked.

"Well, if I'm staying here, there are things I'll need."

"Like?" Jerrik asked, his voice soft.

I glanced his way, then strolled toward his dresser. "Clothes, mainly. Toiletries. We can go to my place—"

"Too dangerous. No way of knowing who else Benjamin has hired."

"All right. Then I guess shopping."

Jerrik grimaced. I didn't blame him. I hated shopping.

"I don't like the thought of being out in the open like that again," he said. "Too many people for me to watch."

I turned toward him and bit my bottom lip. "There is one other option."

"Yeah? What's that?"

He wasn't going to like this. Then again, neither would I. "My friend, Lucy."

His expression darkened. "What about her?"

I couldn't send her to my place. If Benjamin had someone watching it, they'd follow her. And I refused to put Lucy's life at risk. Course, there was a good chance Benjamin had someone on her anyway. But no matter what we did, we risked exposure. And I didn't particularly enjoy the idea of wearing my wedding dress any longer than necessary. "She can bring me some clothes."

"Can we trust her?"

"With my life," I assured him. "Lucy and I go way back. She'd die before betraying me."

"All right. Arrange to meet with her. But we're in and

out. We don't need to run into another of Benjamin's men."

I nodded. "She can also talk to my father."

Jerrik groaned and tipped his head back. "Knew you were going to say that."

"Well. He *is* the alpha. And he's probably worried sick about me right now."

"Yeah. Fine." He sighed, walked over to his nightstand, and pulled out an old flip phone. "This is a burner phone. Hasn't been used yet so no one will know the number. You call Lucy, and that's it. Smash it and throw it in the trash afterward."

I mock-saluted him. "Yes, sir."

His mouth quirked. But without another word, he tossed some sweats onto the bed for me to change into, and strode out of the room, granting me the privacy I hadn't asked for.

"Lucy, would you stop talking for one second and let me—"

Her voice rose another octave. At this point, only dogs could hear her. I slumped against the dresser and rolled my eyes. *One, two, three...* I counted in my head to keep from losing my cool. Lucy, on the other hand, kept ranting. Something about my father, the pack, Benjamin. The sound of his name grated on my nerves. Not that she could sense that over the phone line.

My patience quickly wore thin. "Lucy!" I shouted.

"I mean seriously, Reagan! You should have seen the look on your father's face. And poor Benjamin, don't even get me started on him."

Oh, yes. Poor Benjamin. No doubt he'd played the role of the grieving fiancé well. He seemed the theatrical sort—what with hiring assassins to kill me and all.

Groaning under my breath, I thumped my head against Jerrik's dresser. I loved the girl, but Lord help me, she never knew when to shut the hell up. The moment I'd spoken my name, she'd started off on this tirade. Pretty sure she hadn't yet stopped for a breath.

"And all the guests, they showed up, and you bailed!"

"Lucy, shut the fuck up!" I growled into the phone.

Silence crept over the line. Oh, thank God. Merciful, blessed quiet. For the first time since ringing her, I could hear my own thoughts.

"Reagan—"

"Just stop, all right? It's my turn to talk."

I heard her sigh. "Fine, talk."

"I'm sorry I bailed."

"Damn right—"

"Lucy! Seriously. Shut up and listen to me. I didn't bail because I didn't want to marry Benjamin. I bailed because the bastard put a hit out on me."

I swear, I could hear her blinking. "What the hell are you talking about?"

"Do you remember the guy I met at the club last night?"

"Mmm, tall, dark, incredibly fuckable."

Laughter slipped past my lips before I could stop it. "Yeah, him."

"You slept with him." A statement, not a question.

"I did. But that's not the point."

"How is that *not* the point?"

"He's an *assassin*, Lucy. *The* assassin. The shadow wolf."

Hysterical laughter raced across the phone line. "Wow. I mean, I knew when you called to expect some kind of crazy explanation, but—"

"It's not crazy." I paused and glanced at the wall. "All right. It's beyond insane. But I'm being entirely serious. We slept together last night. And then this morning, he tracked me to the church and told me that Benjamin put out a contract on my life."

"Why?"

"Why not? Guess Gabriel told Benjamin and Christian that marrying me didn't mean they'd gain power in the pack. The marriage was nothing more than the merging of the packs. My father stipulated that the pack hierarchy wouldn't change. And that, in his death, I take over, but Benjamin gets nothing. From what I've learned today, Benny doesn't like that plan."

Silence.

I waited a few more seconds, then straightened with a frown. "Lucy?"

"I'm here," she murmured. "Jesus, Reagan. You're not kidding."

"Nope." I plucked a strange brooch up off Jerrik's dresser and held it up. It looked old. Ancient, in fact. Tarnished as hell, but still beautiful in the right light. "Seems safe to assume that Benjamin knows I'm alive, too. Considering he sent *another* assassin after me not an hour ago."

"What? Are you all right?"

"I'm fine. David, on the other hand..."

"Wait, David? As in David the Assassin?"

Laughter rolled past my lips. "That's what I thought! At least the shadow wolf sounds a little intimidating."

"All right. So Benjamin is playing some twisted game and wants you dead. What about Gabriel? He needs to be made aware of all this. What if Christian is on board with his son's shenanigans?"

I nodded, then turned and gazed out the window. Thick trees blocked the view and shaded the room, likely why Jerrik had chosen it. Private and cool in the summers.

"So, when are you going to tell him?" Lucy asked.

"I'm not."

"What? Are you insane?"

"Nope. You're going to tell him."

"Me?" she squeaked. "You *are* insane. No way in hell I'm going to tell Gabriel that the werewolf he meant for his daughter to wed is trying to kill her. He'll kill *me*."

"Nawh. Maybe maim you, but he definitely won't kill you."

"Gee, thanks."

I snickered at her wry tone. "Don't worry about Gabriel. He's not near as frightening as he pretends."

"Yeah, to *you*. His precious daughter. Why can't you call him?"

"Because if he's with Christian right now, and I call him, Christian will know. And if Christian is in on this with his son, then he'll warn him. That doesn't work with my plan."

"Which would be?"

A slow grin spread across my face. "Oh, it's a very basic plan. I figure killing Benjamin is a good place to start. But if someone warns him ahead of time that I'm on to his plan, he might bail. Where's the fun in that?"

"You know...sometimes you scare me."

"Oh, come on. You love me."

"True. But it's a scary kind of love."

I waved a hand even though she couldn't see it. "Once you talk to my father, I need another favor."

"Mhm. Always something, isn't it? So needy."

God, I loved her. "I need you to meet me and bring some clothes. I needed out of this dress, so Jerrik ripped it off."

"Hot," she said, laughing. "I grabbed your bag from the church. I can bring that to you. It has your phone, too. Where do you want to meet?"

I rattled off an address for a park a few blocks away. Public, but hopefully secluded enough that I'd know if someone followed her. I trusted Lucy, but Jerrik had gone through extremes to keep this place off the radar. I refused to be the person that exposed his home.

"Can do. All right. Talk to your father, let him kill me, and then meet you with clothes. Sounds like a solid plan."

My mouth tugged upward. "Thanks, Lucy. I seriously appreciate this."

"I know. You'd be lost without me. It's all right. You've always been a mess. Now, tell me about this hottie wolf of yours."

"Later!" I said, laughing. "We can gossip at the park."

"Ooh, that sounds fun. I have something to share with you, too."

"You do?"

"You aren't the only one who had fun last night."

I rolled my eyes, unsurprised that Lucy had taken someone home.

"Give me half an hour to talk to your father. I can't imagine that conversation going over well. And then I'll come meet you. So let's meet in an hour?"

I flicked a glance at the clock next to Jerrik's bed. "Sounds great. One hour. Oh, and Lucy? Maybe leave Jerrik's name out of it when you talk to Gabriel. They don't have the best history."

"Of course they don't," she sighed. "You aren't making this easy, are you?"

"Sorry."

"No, you're not. Punk."

"Brat."

We disconnected the call without another word. Part of me felt sorry for Lucy. No one wanted to be the bearer of bad news, and she was about to drop a bomb on Gabriel. I couldn't blame her for worrying. But everyone knew he'd never harm a hair on her head. He'd always jokingly called her his unwanted daughter, but he said it lovingly.

I shattered Jerrik's burner phone and dropped it into the trash as directed before opening the door. He stood on the other side, leaning against the wall in what had to be his favorite position—arms and legs crossed.

"Guess you heard the whole conversation then?" I asked.

His mouth curved upward. "Fuckable, hey?"

"Her words, not mine."

He pushed away from the wall and strode toward me. "Ah. So you don't think I'm fuckable?"

Hearing that word on his lips shouldn't have turned me on. But damn. I licked my lips and lifted a brow. "I didn't say that, either."

"No?" He leaned toward me, his hands braced against the wall next to my head. "Then what would you call me?"

My heart gave a solid kick. I lifted my chin and watched as his wolf came out to play, a hint of gold brightening his eyes. We had to meet Lucy in an hour, but that left some time to spare. I couldn't get last night out of my head. It'd be crazy to turn him down.

Before I could respond, Jerrik dipped his head and kissed me, his mouth fierce and possessive. I sucked in a sharp breath and sank against him, reveling in the feel of his tongue as it stroked mine. He grabbed my hips and held on as he guided us back into his bedroom until the bed met the back of my thighs. Without breaking from the kiss, he turned us and dropped down on the mattress, settling me above him.

"We don't have near enough time for what I want to do to you," he growled. "Next time we'll go slower."

Next time? I loved the thought of him planning ahead, but he didn't give me any time to contemplate *next time*. Instead, he slid his hands under his old sweatshirt and found my breasts. He ran his fingers over my pebbled nipples, a contented smile pulling at his lips.

"Love how you respond to me," he murmured.

I grabbed the hem of the sweatshirt, pulled it off, and

threw it aside. The sweats went next, thrown clear across the room. I really didn't care where.

Grinning down at him, I shifted my hips and rubbed against him, warmth spreading through my stomach when his head fell back and he groaned. He wasn't the only one who loved the responses. His body seemed tuned to mine. Every time I touched him, it was like fireworks for the both of us.

I clawed off his t-shirt and bent over him, running my mouth over every inch of his muscled chest while I removed his belt. I popped open his jeans, then glanced up at him as I shimmied them down. The second I freed him from his jeans, I took his length into my mouth. He didn't taste like chocolate cake, but I found him just as delicious. I started to move, licking and sucking every inch until the sound of his quickened breath made me release him. Once the gold dimmed from his eyes, I returned with a renewed hunger—continuously teasing him until his body went taut beneath mine. I felt his shaft thicken in my mouth, felt his fingers tense in my hair. But every time he approached the precipice, I pulled back. Couldn't let him come, not yet. Punishment for the wonderful torment he'd unleashed upon me last night.

"Jesus woman," Jerrik growled. "Trying to kill me?"

He gripped my hips and rolled us across the bed. He leaned down and kissed me, nipping at my lips and tongue.

"Condom," I murmured against his mouth.

Jerrik leaned over and grabbed one off the nightstand. I licked and kissed his ear and throat while he worked to slide it on. Then I dragged his mouth back to mine, eager to continue. "Now," I whispered.

A wicked smile chased across his face. "Maybe."

"No, now."

"Impatient much?" he teased.

To show him how right he was, I reached down and grabbed him. His lashes fluttered when his eyes closed, reveling in the sensation of me stroking him. He was so close—I'd brought him to the edge with my mouth. Now I wanted to finish him.

His eyes flashed open and with a growl, he thrust. I cried out as he slid within me, my head falling against the pillows. I wrapped my legs around his hips and urged him faster, harder, anything. So long as he didn't stop moving.

Jerrik quickly settled into an unrelenting rhythm, one that ignited a blaze within me. My entire body shuddered around him, my toes and fingers tingling as I neared my own orgasm. He reached down, his fingers working me while he continued to thrust. My orgasm exploded within me. I cried out and rode the waves, my eyes rolling to the back of my head.

"God, I love how that feels," he grunted in my ear. "You tighten around me whenever you come."

Jerrik changed angles, lifting himself up onto his arms, and thrust deeper. The force pushed me back on the bed, the pillows tucked around my head.

"Don't stop," I begged, a second orgasm already starting to build.

I braced my hands against the headboard just as my body lit up once more. I moaned and lifted my hips as I rode out my climax. At the height of my orgasm, I felt Jerrik succumb to his own. His pace shattered and his own cry blended with mine. Once spent, he collapsed next to me on the bed and released a low laugh.

"Amazing," he said, still chuckling.

I smiled and turned my head to look at him. Amazing didn't begin to describe it, but for now, it would suffice.

I TOYED with Jerrik's chest hair and glanced at the clock. It wouldn't take long to reach the location I'd arranged with Lucy, which left us some time to cuddle. Reveling in the moment, I snuggled into Jerrik and ran my fingers down his side. The lower my hand strayed, the quicker his heart beat, a response that almost convinced me to forgo meeting Lucy and initiate the next round. I contemplated it, until my fingers ran over a section of ridged skin. I lifted my head and glanced down, noticing an old scar that wrapped around his side in the shape of what looked like a wolf's mouth.

"What happened here?" I asked.

Jerrik didn't bother lifting his head. "An old injury."

"Obviously," I chuckled. "But how did it happen? Werewolves don't scar unless wounded with silver."

He shifted his weight and rolled onto his side, hiding the scar. "I wasn't always a werewolf."

I nodded. He'd mentioned that before, but I hadn't been able to ask about it, even though I'd wanted to. I met his troubled gaze. Darkness lingered within his eyes, hinting at something unpleasant.

"Hey." I leaned toward him and brushed my mouth against his. "It's all right. You don't need to tell me."

He lingered over my mouth, teasing me with the promise of another kiss before leaning back on his pillows. "I've actually never told this story to anyone. But I like you."

Wow. The simplest statement, but one that left me reeling. Hoping to lighten the mood, I quirked a brow and said, "You like me, huh?"

"The moment I spotted you at the club, I was intrigued."

I rolled my eyes. "Who wouldn't be? I'd just deep-throated a chocolate penis."

His laughter shook the bed. "That certainly helped."

"Men."

"Women," he said with a playful scoff. "Hey. You were the one deep-throating the damn thing. Don't blame me for looking. Still, though. I do like you. I care about your wellbeing. And that's more than I've let myself feel for anyone in a very long time."

All right. Not the direction I'd expected this conversation to head. I snuck him a glance, my teeth worrying at my bottom lip. I'd never given much consideration to relationships. I'd braved a few flings, but they'd never been more than passing fancies. My life was always too busy for that sort of stuff. I didn't love them and leave them—like my dear friend, Lucy—but I never stuck around past a certain point, either. The moment things grew serious, I bailed. I had my reasons. Gabriel, for one. Whoever I dated would have to put up with him. And so few of my pack were willing to try. Those who did, I had to wonder about their motivations. Did they actually like me? Or was it the idea of what I could offer? Those sorts of concerns had long since put a damper on my dating life. It'd always seemed best to cut ties before they hurt me.

But Jerrik?

I didn't want to cut ties with him. And I certainly didn't get the feel that he wanted me for the status. The man had spent his entire existence avoiding the pack. And from the sound of it, he could have easily killed my father and taken over as the alpha. But he hadn't. He'd let Gabriel live. So, if his motivations weren't political, then what the hell was he doing here? What did he want from me? These questions had my pulse racing.

Jerrik pushed the hair back from my face. "You okay? Your heart is pounding."

I forced myself to swallow, then nodded. Talk about freaking myself out. But I needed to calm the eff down. He'd said he'd liked me—not *loved* me. Two very different things. "I'm fine. Don't mind me. You were saying?"

He studied my face. Lord knew what he found, but eventually he continued. "I didn't lie when I said I can't recall my birth year. After time, things start to get muddled up here." He tapped his head. "But there are some things I can't forget, no matter how hard I try. And I doubt I ever will."

"Like when you were changed into a werewolf," I surmised. Few in our pack had been forcibly changed. Gabriel had long-since implemented laws to protect humans from that. To change a human without consent equaled a death sentence.

"That, and other things," he murmured. "Unlike you, I was born human. Oddly enough, I still remember how that felt. I hadn't realized at the time how incredibly mortal we were. My people believed in gods and the mystical, but we had no concept of eternity. And I'd certainly never wondered about werewolves. Back then, there were only two things I cared about: my friend, Leif, and my wife, Tove."

"You were married?" Not sure why that surprised me. He'd led an entire life before meeting me. Hell, he'd probably led twenty. Not that it stopped the green-eyed monster from rearing his head.

Jerrik chuckled and pulled me against him. "Almost a thousand years ago. Doesn't even feel real anymore. Tove and I had known each other since childhood—it'd only seemed natural to marry. Leif I'd met a little later in life, but he quickly became my brother. So, when our people banished him from Iceland, and he decided to travel west, Tove and I agreed to go with him."

*Wait, what?* I pushed up onto my elbows and stared down at Jerrik in astonishment. "Are you talking about Leif Erikson? Your best friend was Leif Erikson?"

Jerrik simply smiled. "Are you going to let me tell my story?"

I blinked, then eagerly nodded.

"Eventually, we came across Greenland, and Leif decided to make it our home. We lived there quite happily. Tove gave me two beautiful children: a daughter we named Eira, and my son, Baldr." Sadness chased across his face. "Unfortunately, a few years after Baldr's birth, a fire ravaged our little colony. I managed to save Baldr, but I lost my wife and daughter."

My chest tightened. And just like that, the green-eyed monster vanished. "I'm so sorry."

Jerrik caught my eye and smiled, though it didn't quite reach his eyes. "It all happened a long time ago. But at the time..." He shook his head. "It felt like my entire world had come crashing down. I felt like the gods had betrayed me. Leif eventually suggested that we sail back to Norway, and I agreed. Anything to leave that damned place. I packed up Baldr and we left. I found myself hoping for a new beginning in Norway. Leif certainly found one. While there, he converted to Christianity, and he convinced me to do the same. I was so mad at Odin for taking everything from me that I didn't think twice. I thought maybe this new religion would be better. Little did I know the gods were listening."

I froze. "What?"

He ignored my question and continued onward. "Leif and I set out on the ocean again, but we didn't make it back to Greenland. Instead, we found *Vinland*. I was ecstatic. I never wanted to return to Greenland. And here was a new land, a new beginning, a new God. What more could I want?"

The hard edge to his voice told me this story was about to take a darker turn.

"Winter passed, and in the spring, Leif suggested we return to Greenland, but I refused. I hated that place. Hated everything it stood for and everything it reminded me of. So, I told him I would remain behind with my son. The night before Leif set sail, I left Baldr with him, and I went for a walk. I needed a few moments to collect myself. To prepare. I never imagined saying goodbye to my brother. I looked up, and I remember seeing such a beautiful full moon. I prayed to my new God to help me find peace and the strength to begin anew with my son.

"But before I could finish, I spotted movement atop a nearby hill. At first, I couldn't make it out, but eventually, the silhouette of this beast took shape. Its hateful eyes blazed in the darkness, and as it stalked toward me, it snarled, and I could see its massive fangs. I remember thinking it had to be Fenrir—son of Loki. My people's stories had often spoken of the massive wolf who would devour Odin whole. But those were just stories, right?"

Jerrik exhaled and paused for a moment before continuing. "No, this was more than a story. This was proof that the gods my people believed in existed. That *Fenrir* existed. The wolf attacked before I could so much as call for help. And it wasn't quick or painless. He dragged out every agonizing second. In that moment, I knew. This was my punishment for turning my back on Odin. For forsaking him and all the other gods. My only hope was to try and die honorably so that Odin would choose me for Valhalla. But I knew my chances were slim. I'd betrayed him. Why would he take me now?

"When the beast finally retreated, I was left staring up at the stars. I waited for death to take me, and while I waited, I picked out all of Tove's favorite constellations. Except, with every passing breath, my heartbeat grew stronger. The bite marks began to stitch closed and my broken bones mended. The sun rose, and I'd survived."

I took Jerrik's hand and ran my thumb over his knuckles.

"That morning, I told myself that Odin had taken pity on me and given me another chance. I'd promised myself I wouldn't waste it, that I would do right by him. I didn't realize how far I'd strayed, but it took me the entire day to reach the village. The moon rose just as I found Leif and Baldr. He'd delayed his launch until I returned. But before I could speak, a terrible pain swept over me. I screamed in agony and dropped to the ground, writhing in the mud. It wasn't until my bones began to snap and twist beneath my flesh that I realized Loki's son had *tricked* me. And when I rose on four legs, my face the mirror image of the same beast who had attacked me, I knew he'd *cursed* me. Loki and Fenrir had turned me into a monster."

A deep-set pain chased across his face. "Overcome with rage, I lost control. I tore through the village, murdering everyone in sight. I couldn't stop, could barely think. And once the sun rose, when I became myself again, I found the face of my sweet son staring up at me with empty eyes. Dead."

A tortured sound escaped my lips. Jerrik glanced my way, then lifted his hand and wiped the tears from my cheeks that I hadn't felt fall.

"Jerrik..." I whispered.

"It was a long time ago. But now you know. The scar on my side was the only one that didn't fully heal over, the first bite when Fenrir attacked."

*Jesus.* It explained so much. No wonder Jerrik hated and killed other werewolves. To him, we were monsters. *He* was a monster. Whoever had attacked him had literally broken him. I leaned down and smoothed his hair back. "For what it's worth, I don't think the gods were punishing you. I think you were just in the wrong place at the wrong time. And you stumbled across a sadistic werewolf."

"You weren't there."

No, I wasn't. And I knew I'd never convince him otherwise. "So, that's why you became an assassin? To rid the world of monsters? That's all we are to you, right?"

He slid his arm around my back and pulled me close. "Not you. You're not a monster."

It all made so much sense now. He didn't think of himself as one of us. And we weren't his people. Tove, Baldr, Eira, Leif, they were his people. And they were all dead. He'd traveled alone for centuries, never part of a pack, never witnessing the love and devotion we possessed for one another. And then he'd met Gabriel with his submit or die attitude. I couldn't imagine surviving a thousand years of such solitude.

"I'm so sorry that happened to you," I whispered. "I wish I could go back and change it."

He kissed my brow, then swung his legs over the edge of the bed and stood. "You and me both. But we need to get going. I'm sure Lucy is out there waiting for us."

Right. Lucy. Benjamin. My problems didn't seem so bad in the grand scheme of things. I had my father, my best friend, my pack...and now I had Jerrik. And he had me. Maybe he'd been alone for the past thousand years, but that all ended now.

I followed him into the bathroom and watched as turned the shower taps. Together, we stepped under the spray, and I felt a strange new sensation overcome me. An overwhelming need to care for and protect him, not that he needed it. I wanted to drag him back to bed and kiss him senseless until he forgot every bad thing that'd ever happened to him.

Huh. Guess that meant I liked him, too. And this time, I had no desire to bail.

# 10

I sat on a swing and pumped my legs, climbing higher and higher. Maybe I was a bit big for it, but it gave me a bird's eye view of the entire park. Not to mention, it was fun. In my spare moments as a child, my mother had taken me to a park near our house. One of the first jungle gym's—and I'd loved it. *Five minutes*, she'd said, *where you can be a kid.* A kid who zipped through the obstacle courses, and hung upside down from the bars. The swing had been my favorite. I'd often wondered if I could swing myself around the top bar. But Amalie had always stopped me before I could manage it.

Wasn't anyone to stop me here today, but I knew better than to try. With age came wisdom, they said. And wisdom dictated that I watch for someone *other* than Lucy. Jerrik stood next to the school, leaning against the brick wall. Every few seconds his gaze would stray to our surroundings and he'd scent the air before glancing back my way.

Lucy was five minutes late. Not unusual for her, but disconcerting nonetheless. My mind spun, contemplating all the ways this might have gone wrong. Maybe Gabriel had refused to let her come to me. Or maybe Benjamin had found her before she could reach my father. So many ways this might have gone tits up.

I shot Jerrik another glance, one he interpreted correctly with a quick shrug.

A few pumps later, and I caught her scent on the breeze. I released the chains and sailed off the swing in a graceful leap.

"Show off," Lucy called out from the park entrance.

I straightened and dusted off my hands. My duffle bag hung over her shoulder. The thought of clean clothes that weren't Jerrik's sweats had me rushing toward her. I wanted my own jeans and fresh underwear.

"I was starting to worry," I said.

Her mouth quirked. "Nothing to worry about."

"So, you talked to Gabriel then?"

She grimaced and removed the bag from her shoulder. "Oh, I talked to Gabriel all right. You're lucky I love you, girl. Could have sworn the man was about to have a seizure. Hey, did you ever notice the vein he gets when he's like extremely pissed?"

I couldn't help but laugh. "That thing was my constant companion as a kid."

"Mmm, I bet. You were always a shit disturber."

"Me?" I rocked back on my heels and eyed my friend. "What about you, Miss Drove Your Father's Car Into a Lake?"

"I don't know *what* you're talking about," she said with the hint of a grin. "I was the perfect angel. Unlike you, who now has a contract out on her life. Thought that damn vein would rupture when I told Gabriel. That man is truly terrifying."

"Nawh. He'd never hurt you. Now, gimme!" I beckoned at the bag.

"All right. Don't get your panties in a twist."

"They're already twisted. That's why I need new ones."

"TMI, Reagan," Lucy said with a chuckle. "I packed a little something extra for you."

I quirked a brow, then took the bag from her and dropped it to the ground. A quick zip revealed a few different articles of clothing, my toiletry bag, and my cell phone. Hallelujah!

"Keep digging," she said.

I rummaged farther in, then froze when my fingers brushed something metal. "You didn't."

"Oh, I did. I snuck into your house just for this."

I lifted my chin and met her stare. My mouth split into a wide grin before I could stop myself. She'd packed my favorite sword, the one I'd named Rory as a kid—don't judge. Young and naïve children did stupid things, including naming their best sword after their first crush. Only Lucy and I knew his name—and I intended on keeping it that way.

"You're the freaking best!" I squealed in excitement. In a rush to hug her, I stumbled over the bag and practically clobbered her. "You shouldn't have risked it, though."

She wrapped her arms around me with a soft chuckle. "It's fine. No one was watching your place, and I figured a girl needed her best guy. Though, looks to me like Rory has been replaced."

Once we parted, I followed her gaze. Jerrik still leaned against the wall, his focus locked on us.

"He's even prettier than I remember," Lucy purred.

"Hey, eyes off my assassin."

"So, that's really him, hey? The shadow wolf? I didn't tell Gabriel about him. I told him I didn't know who was helping you. Not sure he believed me."

"Tell me how that conversation went down."

"Well, he's a bit upset you didn't talk to him before leaving the church. But I think he's more concerned about the developing situation. Christian wasn't with him when we spoke, so that's a huge plus. I have to say, though, it took every ounce of persuasion to convince him not to rip their throats out right now and be done with it. I only managed to get twenty-four hours from Gabriel, though. After that, he says they're dead."

I nodded. Unsurprising. Gabriel had always believed in quick and decisive punishments.

"He's called for a meeting tomorrow night at sundown. He made it sound like it was to discuss the future of the packs—which isn't wrong. But remind me again why we don't want him to just kill them?"

"A good deal of their pack came for the wedding," I

reminded her. "If Gabriel strikes and kills them both, what's to stop Christian's pack from retaliating? Next thing you know, he's started a war between the two packs."

Lucy gave a sage nod. "Right. Makes sense. So, what's the plan then?"

"I'm going to give Benjamin exactly what he wants."

"And that is?"

"Me."

She blinked. "Not following you there. He doesn't want you. Remember?"

"No, but he wants me dead."

She sighed and shook her head. "How much you wanna bet I'm not going to like this plan of yours?"

Jerrik either, I figured, considering I hadn't discussed it with him yet. Not my fault the idea had come to me on the swing. "It's simple. We need to gather as much proof as possible to put before Benjamin's pack. There can't be any doubt, or boom, war. So, Jerrik is going to kill me and collect the reward."

A savage snarl ripped through the park. Geez, even my hair stood on end with that one.

Lucy's wide eyes shot to Jerrik. "I...uh, think you pissed him off? Oh, shit. I mean when Gabriel's mad, you take a few steps back and maybe hide. But *him*? Damn, girl."

I turned around, my breath catching at the sight of his wolf straining to escape. Even from here, I could see the furious glow in his eyes, and a hint of his beast in his elongated jaw line. *Creepy.*

"Obviously, I didn't mean you'd *actually* kill me," I

said, knowing my voice would carry the distance. "I figured that'd be self-explanatory."

"Clearly not," Lucy muttered. "A little more information might help."

"I want concrete proof that Benjamin is the one behind all this. If Jerrik "kills" me, he can collect on the fee. I'll keep out of sight and snap some photos of the pay-off, while Jerrik records the conversation."

"One problem with that, dove," Jerrik growled.

"He calls you *dove*," Lucy murmured as an aside. "How sweet."

"Shut up," I grumbled under my breath before glancing back at Jerrik. "What's wrong?"

"David," he said.

"David?" Lucy asked. "Who's...oh, the other assassin, right."

"He saw me with you," Jerrik commented. He pushed off the wall and strode toward us. "There's a chance he might have reported that back to Benjamin."

My mouth pursed as I contemplated that obstacle. "Do you often report back to the person who hires you if you fail?"

"Couldn't say. I've never failed."

Lucy made a soft sound. "Hear that? He's never failed." She chuckled to herself. "Tell us about the process. How does someone even go about hiring the shadow wolf?"

He cast her a quick glance but didn't answer. Yeah, if I were him, I wouldn't give my business practices away either.

"Sexy *and* silent," Lucy mused. "I like him."

"I don't think the feeling is mutual," I commented. "All right. Let's assume that Benjamin hired them face-to-face. Would it be safe to assume that?"

Jerrik turned back to me, the stern expression softening. "Safe enough."

"So, David and Benjamin *have* met. Which means...*you* and Benjamin have met." For some reason, that bothered me. The thought of the two of them sitting around, discussing my murder in lengthy detail.

"It would also be safe to assume that I have a number to contact once the job has been completed," Jerrik added.

Unnerving to think about. But I didn't doubt Jerrik, not anymore. "Is it common practice to hire a *second* assassin before the first has completed the task?"

"Not if the buyer wants it done fast. Benjamin was adamant that the event take place before the wedding."

"The event," I repeated. "Can we just lay it all out. Call it my death, or whatever."

"So gauche, Reagan," Lucy murmured.

"At least it's honest. Why sugar coat it? They planned my *death*. Just say it, for crying out loud."

"Hey..." Jerrik's fingers curled around my shoulders. He dipped his head and met my gaze. "This was all before I met you. Things are different now."

I nodded. It still burned, though. I'd done nothing wrong. I wasn't some mentally disturbed werewolf who needed to be put down. This entire endeavour was nothing more than a power play. Benjamin didn't like what Gabriel was willing to offer. And like a child whose toy had been taken away, he was lashing out and throwing a temper tantrum to the *nth* degree. It sucked.

"As fascinating as it is to watch you two together, can we get back on track?" Lucy asked. "Jerrik was saying something about this all going down before the wedding. Why before?"

Jerrik shrugged. "Maybe he didn't want to get married, didn't want to go on the honeymoon? I didn't answer. But when there's a rush like that, sometimes the buyer chooses to hire more than one employee, to ensure the task is completed on time. Add a little competition to speed things up. But it's not ideal. Amateurs like David enter the playing field and screw things up."

"So, the only thing we need to worry about is if David has reported his failure back to Benjamin."

Jerrik nodded.

"All right—so, call Benjamin and tell him you were playing Reagan," Lucy suggested. "Luring her into believing her she was safe, and then you killed her. Play it up. Tell him his other assassin almost ruined the entire thing, and that you don't appreciate him hiring competition, especially incompetent ones like David."

A shiver rippled down my spine. When the hell had Lucy become so manipulative?

"It's more than a phone call." Jerrik raked a hand through his short hair and cursed under his breath. "What you're asking for requires a dead body."

"Say what?" I said.

"The agreement was to send him a photo of you dead

to initiate payment. And to bring something with me as proof of death when I came to collect."

"A photo is simple enough," Lucy commented. "We can get creative."

"No, you aren't listening." Jerrik blew out a heavy breath. "When they insist something be brought as proof of death, they mean..."

"A piece of the victim," I whispered, that damn chill returning with a vengeance.

He wouldn't meet my gaze. I couldn't blame him, either. Had he ever done this before? It sickened me to think about it.

"Well, we don't *actually* have to dismember Reagan, or anyone for that matter. So long as Benjamin believes you're bringing *something*, that's all that matters, right?" Lucy said. "Did he stipulate at any time that it needed to be a body part?"

Jerrik frowned. "No, but—"

"There we go, then. You can take something else. Oh!" Lucy sucked in a breath, then dropped to her knees next to my bag and fished out my blade. "Take Rory! Anyone who knows *anything* about Reagan knows she would never willingly part with Rory. He's her baby."

Jerrik blinked, a twinkle of amusement thawing his gaze. "Rory?"

I growled and snatched my sword back from Lucy. "Yes, Rory. Got a problem with that?"

"No, not at all." His mouth quirked as though struggling to bite back laughter.

"And Rory isn't going anywhere. He stays with me."

"Okay... Oh!" Lucy's hands darted beneath my sweatshirt's neckline.

"Hey!" I slapped at her hands.

She fished out my gold necklace—a locket Gabriel had given me many years ago with a picture of Amalie in it. The only time I could ever remember him giving me anything sentimental.

"Take this, then," Lucy said. "She never takes this thing off, and everyone knows that."

I hated the thought of parting with it, but Lucy had a point. I'd never taken it off. Until now. I reached behind my neck and opened the clasp. My mouth twisted, but I handed it over to Jerrik, then cupped my bare throat. I'd been naked many times, but this was the first time I'd ever felt nude. For half a century, I'd worn that necklace in silent remembrance of my mother. Gabriel always refused to speak of her—this was all I had left of her. I never thought I'd part with it.

"You tell Benjamin you couldn't dismember her because then Gabriel would know it wasn't an accident," Lucy continued. "I mean, I assume that was part of the arrangement, right? If Gabriel knew his daughter had been assassinated, it would have ruined everything."

Jerrik turned an appreciative glance her way. Seemed he'd begun to warm up to her. Lucy had that effect on everyone.

"You scare me a little," I told her.

"Hey, you have your sword and muscles, I have my mouth."

I choked back a laugh. Wouldn't be the first time I'd thought that same thing. I weighed Rory in my hand and studied the gleaming silver folds. "In the meantime, I want to pay David another visit."

"What?" Lucy frowned. "Why?"

"Collateral in case Benjamin tries to turn the tables on me. David can confirm Jerrik's story."

Jerrik groaned. "You want me to stand up in front of both packs, admit who I am, and confess that someone hired me to kill their damn alpha's daughter?"

I didn't hesitate. "Yes."

"By the gods, woman. Lucy's right, you *are* insane."

"It's time you stopped hiding, Jerrik," I murmured. "Time to join a pack and see that we aren't the monsters you think we are."

"Reagan..."

I shook my head. "I won't force you to do this. I'm not my father. But I think we both know it's time you put aside your past. It won't be easy. I'm sure there are some in the pack who'd rather see you dead than a member. But if you'll let me, I'd like to help with that."

He shook his head. "It'll never work. You're asking for the impossible. Gabriel will challenge me the second he sees me, and I'll kill him."

"What if he doesn't?"

"Doesn't challenge me? Considering how things went down the last time I saw him, I don't see that happening."

"Jerrik—"

"Uh, guys?" Lucy chimed in. "Maybe this is a conversation for a different time? We're under a time crunch remember? And there's a lot to do before meeting Benjamin."

I nodded and dropped the issue, not that it helped to

quiet my thoughts. In the span of twenty-four hours, I had to find David, fake my death, and confront Benjamin in front of his entire pack, all while initiating a truce between my father and Jerrik. If I failed in any of those things, I'd lose my shadow wolf—and I wasn't ready to say goodbye yet.

I EYED THE GLISTENING ROAD, wet with rain, and contemplated our options. Upon returning to Jerrik's, we'd noticed three of Benjamin's dumbass lackeys hiding in and around his neighbors' yards. Spying, most likely. Question was: how had they found his place? Jerrik had kept it a secret for so long. Yet, here they were. Which had led to one massively pissed off assassin. After ten minutes of arguing, we'd given Lucy Jerrik's personal number, then sent her home. She couldn't be seen with us—not if this was going to work.

"You ready for this?" Jerrik whispered in my ear.

Ready to fake my death? Not entirely. If word somehow spread, and Gabriel believed it to be true, he'd raze the town in search of Benjamin. We'd contemplated a quick phone call to let him know the plan, but Lucy had suggested leaving him in the dark. Not only would a real reaction be best if news did spread, but also because she knew my father would try to talk me out of this. If he ordered me not to and I did it anyway, I'd have to be punished for disobeying my alpha. None of us wanted that. Best to err on the side of caution.

"Reagan?" Jerrik whispered.

I nodded. I didn't relish the thought of killing, but these three had to go. My father certainly wouldn't let them live once he handed out Benjamin's death sentence. And if they caught wind that Jerrik and I were staging my death, they'd ruin everything when they reported back to Benjamin. Incapacitating them certainly wasn't an option. Unconscious werewolves didn't remain unconscious for long. It was an added risk we didn't need to take. On the upside, these were the sort of assholes I didn't want in my pack.

"I count three," I said. "One in the yard left of your place. One across the way, next to the apple tree. And one to our right, leaning against his shitty car."

Jerrik's grunt confirmed my count. "We take them out as quickly and quietly as possible, then lug them around to my backyard."

"And get Lucy to phone in a clean up-crew afterward."

He nodded. "We split up. I take the two on my left. You take the one on the right."

"What? Why do you get two and me one?"

Jerrik rolled his eyes. "You really want to argue about this right now?"

I flashed him a wink. "I'm teasing. You can take all three if you want."

"Gee, thanks. You take Ms. Patter's."

Ms. Patter, hey? I turned toward her garden and eyed the path between two rows of gold magnolias. Nice display. Hopefully I didn't ruin it.

"I'm thinking...pizza for dinner," I commented.

Jerrik shot me a startled look. "You're thinking about food right now?"

"Sure." I shrugged. "We're gonna be hungry after all this."

His shoulders shook with laughter. "Why am I not surprised?"

"If I ordered all meat and pineapples, would you eat that?"

"You can pretty much slap anything on a crust, and I'd eat it."

Knew I liked him.

"The rain will help us," Jerrik commented, his gaze scanning the immediate area. "It'll help block our scents, especially if we come at them from downwind. But if they hear us splashing through puddles..."

"Gee, you'd think I'd never hunted before."

Jerrik shot me an amused grin. "All right then, smarty pants. You ready?"

I nodded. Jerrik did the same, then hunkered low and stripped. Seconds later, Jerrik's body shuddered and a massive black wolf took shape beside me. It'd happened so quickly. One moment, I crouched next to a man, and the next a beast. And not a single bone broken. Like magic.

I'd never seen anything quite so beautiful. Every other werewolf labored through the shift, groaning as agony tore through our bodies. He stood, his monstrous form towering over me in the bushes—at least six feet tall. Were it not for the giant cypress tree standing sentinel before us, Jerrik's wolf form would have given away our position.

He shook out his fur, then swung his head around, his startling amber eyes connecting with mine.

Unable to resist, I lifted a hand and ran it over his smooth coat, my fingers threading through the soft black fur. No mistaking why they called him shadow wolf. Not a single colored tuft marred his dark as night fur. In fact, the only anomaly was the jagged slash across his lip.

He nudged me with his nose, then gestured to the road, as though to say *you coming?* I shed my own clothing and relinquished myself to my wolf. I heard the pleased howl in my head. It slipped past my lips in a long groan as my bones snapped and my body contorted. Whatever magic Jerrik had, it wasn't the same as mine. Every shift was a lesson in torment. One I'd learned to accept many moons ago.

After a moment's pause, I rose on my own four legs and staggered to the side. Jerrik brushed his shoulder against mine and steadied me. I shook out my head, then nodded and turned toward Ms. Patter's yard. Keeping out of range, I crept through the hedges, painfully aware that I was tramping what looked like "award-winning" flowers. Maybe we could send her a note afterward, apologizing.

The first jackass meandered aimlessly among the backyards. Personally, I was surprised no one had bothered to phone the police yet. Strange men lurking in backyards tended to draw much unwanted attention. Maybe Ms. Patter wasn't home?

I crouched low and snuck a glance toward Jerrik. He'd deemed the second jackass leaning against his car as the more important target. I watched as he crept up behind him. All three were completely ignorant of our approach. Quite telling, really. These three were certainly members of Benjamin's pack. Untrained, unskilled, and unwanted. After this whole mess, I really couldn't see Gabriel rolling out the welcome mat, especially if this was their sort of mettle. We'd kill their alphas, then send the rest of the pack home with a hard-learned lesson.

The dumbass in front of me did another lap, leading him around to the side of the house where I waited. A few more steps and he'd spot me. Not that it mattered. I wouldn't let him utter a word. Sure enough, the second he darkened my presence, I leapt, perfectly in sync with Jerrik's own attack.

Soundless and perfectly executed. No snarls like some of my more excitable brothers and sisters. No yips or growls. Nothing but a perfect arc as I sailed through the air, and ripped out his throat. Jackass dropped to the ground in a twitching heap, his blood staining the verdant grass and some lilac-colored thymes.

A stout cry caught my attention and I leaned around the corner in time to catch Jerrik's teeth latch around the third dumbass's thigh. From the looks of it, he'd actually tried to run. Guess that was the smarter option. A monstrous beast like Jerrik didn't go unnoticed. Not sure I would have run, but these men were far from trained. More like Benjamin's underpaid lackeys.

I clamped my teeth around the ankle of the idiot I'd killed and heaved him through the grass and around the back of the house. A massive stone fence stood between the two properties. Made me wonder who'd built it and why. Jerrik, because he liked his privacy, or Ms. Patter because she lived next to a werewolf. Both scenarios had merit.

I tossed the bastard over the fence, and quickly followed after. Jerrik stood in the middle of his yard, his black coat shining in what little sunlight cut through the bruised clouds. We were drenched, both in rain and blood. Tearing out a man's throat was hardly a clean job. But his fur gleamed in the rain, the droplets curling his fur. I huffed under my breath and gestured to the front where we'd shifted. We retrieved our clothes and my duffel bag before returning to his backyard. Once hidden next to the hideous wall, I shifted and threw my clothes back on, shaking off the rainy chill.

Jerrik had finished first and paused in his task to look me over. "You're all right?"

I nodded, then helped him position the bodies near the back fence line, hidden in his own little forest. Somewhere no one would come looking until Lucy dispatched a cleaning crew. With luck, we'd finish the remaining tasks tonight, and I'd enjoy another night in Jerrik's arms before facing down more than one big bad wolf tomorrow evening.

An hour later, I watched as the clean-up crew plucked the bodies out of Jerrik's backyard and loaded them into a truck. I knew they used magic to keep things hidden from view of humans, but other than that, I hadn't a clue how they did their job. And honestly, I never wanted to know. They had their job, I had mine.

One that had me standing in Jerrik's living room as he and I pondered exactly how to kill me. I'd suggested staging me on my back so the photo caught my face. Jerrik aimlessly nodded, his fingers drumming against his thighs as he considered whatever thoughts were whirling around in that head of his.

I'd just about given up trying to read his face when I caught the sound of something small padding toward us. I turned and grinned at the sight of a handsome long-haired cat, his fur the color of a creamsicle. *Oh, my God.* Jerrik had a *cat*. For some reason, that tickled my fancy. The big bad shadow wolf had a feline companion.

With the sophisticated air most cats possessed, he trotted toward me, his tail high in the air as he brushed his cheek against my fingers.

"Hey there, sweet baby," I crooned to him as I hefted the overweight beast up into my arms. "Aren't you handsome?"

The corners of Jerrik's mouth curved. "He knows it, too."

"I can't believe you have a cat. What's his name?"

Jerrik met my gaze, his expression stern and dead serious. "Catsanova."

I couldn't help it. I burst out laughing, hugging the

cat close to my chest as my entire body shook with amusement. "Catsanova? Seriously?"

"Of course." Not a hint of playfulness warmed his voice. "Look at him. He's a lady-killer."

"Who takes care of him when you're away?"

"Ms. Patter next door. She adores him probably more than I do."

If anyone ever bothered to ask—this was the moment. Right here. When I knew I cared for Jerrik more than a little. With his cat tucked up under my throat, my fingers scratching under his furry chin. Warmth spread through my entire body as I held Jerrik's gaze, a soft smile pulling at my lips.

I leaned forward and brushed my mouth against his, breathing in his scent and savoring the moment. The stories I'd heard growing up of the shadow wolf didn't equate to the man standing before me. The stories had painted him as a cold-hearted bastard, but I knew better. I knew the pain within, knew that he was so much more than the assassin the tales made him out to be. And I wanted so much more with him—a notion that terrified the absolute hell out of me.

Jerrik kissed me again, then gestured toward the kitchen. "Dining room table, I think."

Made sense. Benjamin had insisted my death look like an accident. Not only did that limit our options, but locations as well. On the middle of the floor would have suggested a struggle, but the dining room table suggested a peaceful passing. Choking on food, or succumbing to poison—not that poison screamed peaceful.

I lowered Catsanova down and took the furthest seat

from the window, facing the outside. The sun had set hours ago, casting Jerrik's backyard into one long shadow. Part of me wondered if something lingered back there—but the logical part of my brain told me that was just my fear talking. We would have heard anything moving around back there.

"Lean over and lay your head on the table," Jerrik suggested.

I did as he asked and rested my cheek against the cold marble top.

"Good. Now, let go of every bit of tension in your body. Let your arms hang down. Imagine every bit of stress lifting from your shoulders. Light as a feather. Eyes open, though."

Right. I blinked them open and caught his gaze, my mouth quirking as he crouched low next to me.

"Stop that," he murmured.

I lifted a quizzical brow. "Stop what?"

"Watching me like that. You're distracting me."

"And we can't have that," I teased.

Jerrik sighed and covered my face with his palm. "Take a deep breath. No smiling, no looking at me. Stare straight ahead. Wipe your face clean of all emotion."

Which was harder than it sounded. Essentially, *think dead*. An unnerving thought.

"Ready?"

"Yes," I whispered.

His hand vanished. I centered my gaze on the couch, focusing on the tiny imperfections in the lush leather set. *Don't blink.* Of course, thinking about it made me *want* to blink. My eyes dried, and I would have laughed if

Jerrik hadn't moved into my periphery with his phone out.

He moved in a quick circle, snapping photos from all sorts of directions. Were it not so creepy, I might have compared this to a fashion shoot.

"Okay," he finally commented.

I blinked and worked out my jaw as I pushed up from the chair.

He tapped his phone and started running his finger over the screen. "I found an app that lets me modify images."

"Modify how?"

He frowned as he peered at the screen. "Right now, I'm adding a bit of white to your face. To make you look paler. Maybe darken the skin under your eyes?" He pursed his mouth and shook his head. "No. That won't work. Just whitening your skin. Too much color in your cheeks otherwise. There. Should be good."

"Let's see."

"You sure?"

I nodded. If we were going to do this, it had to be done right. I wanted to make sure there weren't any mistakes that would give us away.

He handed over his phone, and my breath caught at the sight of me, dead. A shiver tore down my spine and the hair on the back of my neck stood up. For a phone app, it'd definitely done the job. I looked, for all intents and purposes, dead. It wasn't a look I wore well. "Wow."

"Yeah, a bit unnerving." Jerrik took the phone back and growled under his breath. "I'll fire this image off to the burner phone, and then send it to him from there."

"Give me about ten minutes first. I need to call someone in the pack first to get a bead on David, in case word does spread about my death. When he grabbed me, I could smell my pack on him. He's definitely a member."

"Oh. That's not going to end well."

"Nope." Gabriel would make an example of him in front of everyone. Personally, I'd be there to watch with a smile on my face.

All these steps and precautions, but I knew it'd be worth it in the long run. I scooped up Catsanova and pressed my face against his. Seeing myself like that...I felt cold inside. It didn't seem so amusing anymore that someone wanted me dead. Not that it'd amused me before. But that image had made it seem far too real.

"Don't worry, baby," I murmured to Catsanova. "I'm not going to let Benjamin win."

"Damn straight," Jerrik snarled as he rubbed a comforting hand down my arm.

I watched as he sent the photo to his burner phone in preparation, the apprehension in the air palpable. Either Benjamin fell for this, or he didn't. Regardless, only one of us was coming out of this—and it sure as hell was going to be me.

"Once you send him the picture, how long until he gets back to you?"

"Shouldn't be long," Jerrik commented. He wrapped an arm around my shoulders and pulled both me and Catsanova into his chest. I leaned my head against his shoulder, enjoying the moment for as long as I could before reality set back in.

"And when he does?"

"He'll set up a time and location to meet. Probably early morning, after midnight type thing. A lot of these guys don't understand that nighttime is far more conspicuous. You see two guys meeting in the middle of the day, you don't think to look twice. You see two guys meeting at night..."

"And suddenly you're jotting down their full description to relay to the cops."

He nodded. "All right. You go call whoever it is you need to call. And in a few minutes I'll send this photo off to Benjamin. Ready?"

"Ready."

"Break."

I grabbed my phone and started for his room, my mouth splitting into a wide grin when Jerrik patted my ass as I sauntered by.

# 12

I WOKE when the mattress shifted beneath me. Blinking open my eyes, I bit back a yawn and glanced up at Jerrik. Shit. I hadn't meant to fall asleep. I'd phoned Ana—the woman responsible for keeping track of every pack members' home and work addresses, cell phones, emails, etc.—and afterward, laid back on the bed. Just to rest my eyes, I'd told myself. What with the wedding, the assassination attempt, my romp in the sack with Jerrik, and all the subsequent shifting, I must have drifted off after receiving David's address.

I shot a glance at my phone tucked in amongst the rumpled covers and cursed. I hadn't meant to nod off.

"Damn it." I snatched my phone and lit up the screen. Holy shit. Countless missed phone calls, voicemails, text messages. My breath hitched in my throat as I scrolled through the many missed notifications. "I think it's safe to say word definitely spread."

Jerrik nodded. "Lucy called. About an hour ago, an anonymous person called your father and informed him of your death. It didn't end well."

Tears sprang to my eyes. This had been part of the plan. I *knew* that. But I also knew how my father would react.

"A half an hour later, Benjamin phoned and challenged your father. The fight is scheduled for eight o'clock this morning."

That moved up our timeline considerably. Guess Benjamin didn't want to wait. "Why didn't you wake me?"

Jerrik shook his head. Shadows darkened the underside of his eyes. "Because I didn't want you to know until you absolutely needed to. Letting you sleep seemed best."

My fingers tightened around my phone as I stared down at it. The LED light flashed at me, urging me to check my messages, but I couldn't. I couldn't let them show that they'd been read.

"It'll be all right," Jerrik murmured, his voice so soft in the silent house. "I sent that photo off a while ago. Benjamin thinks you're dead so there won't be any more surprise attacks."

"Yes, but my *father* also thinks I'm dead. Along with everyone else."

He nodded, his face softening in the dim light. "I'm truly sorry you're going through this. But it'll all be over soon."

I lifted my chin. "And then what?"

His jaw tightened, and he didn't say a word. What I would have given to be able to read his mind. My pulse raced as I imagined the rest of my life without him. We'd only known each other a little while, but I wanted more. I wanted to ask if he did too, but fear caged my tongue.

"Come on, we need to go." Jerrik pushed to his feet. "Benjamin wants to meet in forty-five minutes. I'd like to arrive first so we can scope out the best spot for you."

"What about David?"

"We'll track him down after. Did you get the address?"

I nodded, then shot another glance at my phone. "What..." My voice drifted off.

"What, what?"

I shook my head and tried again. "What about my body? Doesn't my father want to collect it?"

"Very much so. Benjamin sent him the photo of you. I'm sorry—I never imagined he'd stoop so low. Lucy said he's ordered his personal guard to find you."

His personal guard. Jesus. "He's without protection right now?"

"I don't think he cares, Reagan."

Holy shit. "He's going to get himself killed!"

"Benjamin has already issued the challenge. No one else can challenge your father until that first one is dealt with. And we plan to be there before that happens, right?"

"I need to call him." I nodded and lifted my phone. "He can know I'm all right. I'll tell him what we're doing. Then he'll be fine."

"Not the time, dove," Jerrik said, his hand coming to rest on mine. "What if Christian is with him? Not to mention, that's not a thirty-second phone call, and we need to go. Your father will be fine once he sees you. In the meantime, he needs to think you're gone. His reactions need to be honest."

"He'll hate me for putting him through this," I whispered.

Jerrik's arms slipped around my waist and he pulled me into his chest, his lips pressed to my brow. "Your father could never hate you. I just need you to hold on a little bit longer, all right?"

Though my bottom lip quivered, I sucked in a deep breath and nodded.

"We'll get through this next part with Benjamin, then we'll find David, and then we're off to see your father. Nice and easy."

Right. Easy. Except that every bone in my body wanted to destroy Benjamin. A part of me didn't care about first proving him guilty, or having the packs' consent to deliver justice. I wanted to run Rory through his heart and spit on him when he fell curled around my blade.

I had to keep it together, though. There were laws for a reason. Measures set in place to ensure people didn't walk around killing each other. If I killed Benjamin before the two packs ruled him guilty, I'd go up in flames as well.

But once the packs proclaimed him guilty—and they would—I had every intention of killing his cowardly ass.

AT FOUR-THIRTY IN THE MORNING, I should have been in bed, snuggled up against Jerrik. Instead, I was perched in a building across from the arranged location, crouched in a half-open window. Benjamin had chosen the industrial center, which had made Jerrik laugh and shake his head. Apparently, Benjamin was a rank amateur in his eyes. People didn't pay in large cash drops anymore. Too easy to track. But, for the sake of the plan, it didn't matter. I had no intentions of keeping the money, and neither did Jerrik—too creepy to even think about.

We had three goals here tonight. Successfully capture Benjamin on Jerrik's voice recorder explicitly discussing the contract, take a few photos of them talking together, and assuage any concerns Benjamin might have about my death. The most important thing here was for him to believe Jerrik had killed me.

When I asked if Jerrik had a copy of the contract, he merely smiled. Apparently, things like this were agreed upon verbally. Neither party signed anything. When I'd asked why, he'd shrugged and asked what a contract would do for them? If either party refused to follow through, waving a piece of paper in the air wouldn't solve matters. So, what was the point in signing something? Which meant my plan would have to suffice. Photos, recordings, and another witness. We *needed* one other person to back up our story. Otherwise, Benjamin's pack could claim we'd forged the evidence.

No room for error.

Unfortunately, I had very little light up here to snap

any photos. Sometime throughout the night, a swath of thick clouds had rolled in, cutting off the moonlight. The only remaining light belonged to a streetlamp next to the meeting spot. And from up here, that light wouldn't be enough. One glance at my camera and I knew the pictures would come out grainy at best.

That was a slight problem.

Cursing under my breath, I slunk away from the window and bolted through the room, then rushed down two flights of stairs. I paused near the exit and lifted my nose in the air. If Benjamin was smart, he'd bring his own men. Someone to guard his back while the payment took place. I couldn't pick up anything other than the scent of the impending storm on the horizon. Which meant, either Benjamin and his men weren't here yet, or they were upwind from me.

I leaned around the edge of the building and caught sight of Jerrik. He stood in the middle of the street, his hands jammed in his pockets—a stance meant to lure people in, see him as harmless. The thought made me laugh.

Jerrik shifted his weight in my direction. A sign he'd heard me maybe? I didn't have time to ask. I shot across the street and leapt into the air, my feet and fingers scrambling for purchase against a stone wall. Once at the top, I ran across it, then leapt onto the nearest parking structure roof and placed myself downwind from Jerrik.

At first glance, the light seemed brighter. So, I dropped down onto my stomach and quirked an ear. I caught the sound of Jerrik's feet as he paced back and forth, and distantly, the sound of a car rolling up.

"He's here," I said, knowing Jerrik would hear me now.

He grunted under his breath.

Pulling my phone out of my pocket, I dimmed the screen and activated the camera app. I switched to night mode, made sure the flash was off, then belly-crawled to the edge of the roof and snapped a shot of Jerrik. Not as clear as day, but nowhere near as grainy as the photos from the other building. This location would suffice.

Footsteps approached.

I flattened down and held my breath as I listened. From the sound of it, Benjamin had brought two others with him. Worse case scenario, we'd kill all three and deal with the pack later. I really wanted to avoid that, though. We were the victims. I needed to keep it that way.

"Evening, Jerrik." Benjamin's posh accent carried through the light breeze.

My lip curled the moment I heard it. At least across the street, I wouldn't have had to listen to him, but I didn't have that advantage here. And boy, did the sound of his voice invoke a serious rage within me. My wolf surged up in the back of my mind, ready to howl its displeasure for everyone to hear.

I swallowed the damn beast and squeezed shut my eyes. This wasn't the time nor place. I refused to be the reason the two packs went to war. We would decimate them, but we'd lose many good people in the process. Not the way I wanted things to go down between us.

"I must admit, I was surprised when I received your text."

Jerrik snorted under his breath. "We have a contract,

don't we?"

"We do. But word around the water cooler is you had a change of heart."

Silence crept through the night. We'd expected this. David would have ratted Jerrik out the first chance he had. But Jerrik had the play the part.

"Change of heart," Jerrik repeated. "Not what I'd call it."

"I heard you were at the church."

"You wanted it done before the wedding, didn't you? Wouldn't have made sense to let her walk down the aisle."

"Or, you could have done it last night when you saw her at the club. Before you two went home together."

I tensed. Of course someone had been watching me. I cursed inwardly and dropped my head against the chilled cement. Why hadn't I seen that coming?

"What, you wanted me to kill her right then and there in the middle of the club? Wouldn't have looked much like an accident, would it? You wanted her dead. The bitch is dead. You planning on standing out here questioning me all night? I'm freezing my fucking balls off."

*Colorful.* Though, I had to admit, it definitely drove home the point.

"That was your whole plan then? Sleep with her, then kill her?"

A frosty laugh slipped past Jerrik's lips. "Think it's my first time making a woman come before watching the light leave her eyes?"

Even I shivered with that one. And I hoped to God it

wasn't true. Might make me question everything I knew about Jerrik. Though that chill didn't compare to the one that shot down my spine when Benjamin laughed. Anyone who could laugh at that... Yup, I definitely wanted to carve out his heart. Maybe stomp on it a little. Okay, a lot.

"So, outside the restaurant? Just more of your silly game?" Benjamin asked.

"No, that's called collateral damage. It's what happens when some asshole hires a *second* assassin to do the *same* job. You're lucky that jackass didn't blow everything for me."

"He claims—"

"Look, I honestly don't give two shits what he claims. He's lucky he's alive, pulling a stupid stunt like that. And I'm done playing this game with you. Reagan is dead like you wanted. Maybe I took her out for a spin once or twice, but what do you care? You weren't banging her. And the bitch was attractive for a soon-to-be dead chick. So, pay up. Some of us want to get some shut-eye before the damn sun comes up. We don't all have a big showdown happening later this morning."

I shook my head and released a slow breath. If it weren't for his voice, I wouldn't have thought that was Jerrik. He sounded like a completely different person here. Cold, callous. And nothing like the man I'd come to know. It had to be an act. But part of me wondered, which was his real face?

"All right, mate. Don't go losing your head," Benjamin chuckled. "You got something else to show me?"

"You mean this ugly thing?"

With a deep breath, I slowly crept up to the edge and glanced over. Jerrik held up a fist. Dangling from his clenched fingers was my locket. The thought of Benjamin touching my treasured possession made me sick. I'd worn that necklace for half a century. Kept it close to my heart as a way to remember my mother. I didn't want to turn that over to him as some sick trophy.

Benjamin's laughter rose and he reached for it. "Maybe I'll ransom it back to Gabriel—you know, before I kill him."

Jerrik snatched it back. "Don't think so, *mate*. I'm keeping it."

I had to swallow my gasp.

"You're...what?"

Jerrik held it up to the moonlight and studied the spinning trinket. "Add it to my own trophy collection. Need something to remember this kill by."

"Our deal—"

"You got what you wanted," Jerrik snarled, his power flaring. Even I felt the surge. "If you want the necklace, come and take it from me."

Benjamin blinked first, then dropped his head and snapped his fingers at one of his lackeys. Someone strode across the pavement, their steps a bit uneven. Benjamin snatched a large duffel bag from one of his goons and started handing it over to Jerrik.

My mouth pinched as I brought out my phone and snapped a few photos, just in time to catch the handoff. Benjamin turned back to his goons, his profile to me. I held down the button on my phone, and let it snap as many photos in a sequence as it would allow.

Jerrik opened the bag and glanced inside. Apparently appeased by what he saw, he nodded and zipped it up. "Guess we're done here. Would like to say it's been a pleasure, but it really hasn't."

Benjamin's mouth curled into a nasty grin. "When I take over the pack today, I expect you there to proclaim your loyalty. Show the two packs that the shadow wolf obeys me."

A short burst of laughter rolled past Jerrik's lips. "You know, you're a lot like Gabriel. He demanded the same thing of me five hundred years ago." I watched in awe as Jerrik's eyes slowly ignited, the gold rolling over his pupils. Standing out in the darkness, he looked like a wild animal. "It didn't go so well for him then, can't imagine it would go well for you."

Benjamin opened his mouth, but Jerrik silenced him with a sharp snarl. "Might wanna think before you open that mouth of yours. Being out this late puts me in a sour mood."

I almost gasped when Benjamin snapped his jaw shut. *Holy shit*. It was the first time I'd seen Jerrik express his alpha status. He'd only warned Benjamin, but even I'd felt the power of his words wash over me.

"Move, now," Benjamin snapped at his men. "Until next time, shadow wolf."

"Oh, and Benjamin?" Jerrik commented, his voice eerily calm. "I wouldn't expect to be hearing back from those thugs you stationed at my house if I were you. Won't even ask how you knew where I lived, but feel free to assume I wasted them. Darken my doorstep again and I'll paint my street red, if you get my drift."

Benjamin's upper lip curled back. Unfazed, Jerrik turned and stalked off into the darkness.

I waited for Benjamin and his men to peel out in their car before I pushed to my feet and raced across the rooftops. A few blocks later, I jumped down onto the street and came face to face with Jerrik.

Standing close to him, my entire body instinctively reacted. It wasn't often I felt overwhelmed by an alpha's power. I'd suffered my father's wrath a few times growing up, but that hardly compared to now. Every hair on my body stood on end and my skin prickled. The werewolf within wanted me to drop to my knees before him and expose my throat—but I refused. I would never bow to Jerrik, or anyone for that matter.

"Jesus," I whispered, rubbing my hands up and down my arms before gesturing at his face. "How about dimming the headlights a little? You're blinding me."

"Sorry," he grunted, a hard edge darkening his voice. He closed his eyes and drew in a full breath of the night air. When he released it and opened his eyes, his baby blues stared down at me. "That guy pisses me off."

The corner of my mouth quirked. I'd guessed that already.

"I have the money. Let's find David and finish this."

I nodded, but before either of us moved, I cupped his chilled cheek, rose onto my tiptoes, and brushed my mouth against his. A brief kiss, but one that seared my soul. "I know that was hard for you. So thank you."

"I hated every second of that. Knowing you could

hear me. But I had to... That's not who I am, Reagan."

I nodded and slipped my arms around his neck. "I know."

"And I never...I would *never* murder someone after sleeping with them."

Relief washed through my muscles. I wish I hadn't needed to hear those words, but guess I did. Regardless of my feelings for him, we didn't know one another all that well yet. I knew only a fraction of his long history. I knew how he'd become a werewolf, but what about those thousand years since? His reassurance soothed that little knot in my gut.

Jerrik cupped the back of my head with his free hand and dragged me into his chest. Tension ran through his entire body, his fingers tightening in my hair as he breathed in my scent. Guess I wasn't the only one stressed out.

With a soft sound, I nuzzled his neck and ran my lips down his throat, savoring this quiet minute while waiting for his wolf to settle. Knowing I had that effect on him was addictive.

"We need to go. But first..." He brushed my hair back and fastened my locket around my neck. "I saw your face when Lucy took this from you, and couldn't stand the thought of his greasy fingers all over it."

My cheeks burned with unspent tears. I wouldn't cry. I *wouldn't*. I lifted my hand and touched my necklace. "Thank you."

"Of course." He leaned in and brushed a kiss against my brow, then stepped back. "All right. Let's get going. We still need to find David."

Well, this part wasn't going quite as well. I tapped my index finger against my hip and stared up at the quaint house. As far as houses went, it seemed like any other. Sturdy walls, windows, a garage...but it lacked the distinct werewolf scent that tended to give away our locations. Either David hadn't come home in the past month, or...

"He gave the wrong address," Jerrik growled.

I nodded. That definitely seemed more plausible. And far more intelligent than I would have thought. David didn't seem like a smart cookie, since he'd attacked me in broad daylight outside a restaurant. A lack of foresight and ability to think beyond the moment. But if he'd lied to us, then it seemed safe to assume he did, in fact, have a brain. Not that this line of thought helped us in the slightest. Time was running out. After stashing the money somewhere safe and backing up our phones as a precaution, we'd headed here. But it'd taken long enough that the sun had already risen, peeking out from behind the thick clouds.

"So, now what?" I asked.

Jerrik marched up the sidewalk and banged on the front door, practically rattling the entire house. I winced, and glanced around. The sun might have risen, but that hardly meant everyone else had.

He lifted his fist, about to pound again when the sound of shuffled steps drew our attention.

"Someone's coming," I told him.

The wooden door creaked open and through the screen, an old lady peered up at Jerrik. My mouth tugged at the sight of her, all messy rollers and thick glasses resting low on her nose. Her frumpy nightgown was something I aspired to when I reached that age—flannel and flowered and hideous.

"Young man, have you any manners?" she warbled in a weathered voice. "Do you know what time it is?"

We did. Sadly. Every second counted. I jogged up the sidewalk and plastered a happy smile on my face before unleashing it on her. "Oh." I blinked for effect. "We're so sorry! We must have the wrong address." I pretended to lean back and study the rest of the cul-de-sac. "I could have sworn he said he lived here, though."

I turned back to the old woman. "We're so sorry for disturbing you. My goodness, how embarrassing! My husband here never wants to ask for directions, you know?"

Jerrik shot me a glance, one fitting of my faux hubby.

The old woman threw me a toothy smile. "Men, darling. They wouldn't stop and ask for help even if it saved their lives."

"So true. But while I'm here, you wouldn't happen to know someone by the name of David Taylor, would you? I could have sworn this was his address."

"David Taylor is the sweet young man who sold me this house," she offered. "Handsome lad. Very polite."

Polite enough to hold a blade to my throat, sure. But arguing that point was a waste of time. I nudged Jerrik. "See, honey. You just need to ask the right questions."

He grunted and folded his arms over his chest.

"Oh, stop sulking. You did find the right address, after all." I caught the woman's stare and shook my head, playing up my role. "Men, right? You wouldn't happen to have David's forwarding address, would you?"

"Of course, dear. Used to be everyone knew where everyone else lived, back in my day. But those interwebs now keep everything a secret." She rambled as she shambled toward her kitchen.

I almost burst out laughing. I definitely aspired to be her when I was old. Though, I had a long way to go before that day came. Still, I couldn't wait to patter around my old house, ranting about the crazy days before the interwebs. Little did she know, I actually pre-dated both her and the Internet.

She snatched a slip of paper off her refrigerator and shuffled back toward us. "Here you go, dear. It's not very far. Shouldn't take long. I recall him mentioning that he liked the neighborhood but didn't need such a large place for just him. Me, my children and grandkids love to visit here, so the space gives them room to play. It's only me now, though. My dear husband passed, oh, about a decade ago, now?" She fiddled with her glasses. "He would have given your man here a run for his money in the looks department. Quite the looker, my George. You would have found him handsome."

I bit back my laughter. "The address?"

"Right." She lifted her arm, her wrinkled hand closed around something.

I reached out and she dropped the object into my palm. Something solid and...hot. My skin sizzled, the flesh searing. I cried out and threw it to the ground, then jumped backward, shaking out my hand.

Jerrik rushed toward me, his eyes pure gold as he latched onto my wrist and studied my palm. Blisters covered the inside of my hand and weren't healing.

*What the fuck?*

Snarling under his breath, Jerrik whipped around, about to lunge after the old woman, but instead came to a dead stop. I glanced up to find her standing in the middle of her doorway, a wicked looking pistol gripped between her unsteady hands.

"Silver bullets, dear," she commented.

I glanced down on the porch and, yup. She'd literally handed me a silver bullet. Distracting us long enough to grab her gun. Who the hell was this woman? The Terminator's grandmother? And here I thought we'd had a connection. *Just goes to show, you can't trust anyone in this world.*

"Might want to think this through," Jerrik growled, his voice painfully deep. "You can shoot me, but it better be in the heart or the head. Miss, and I'll rip your throat out."

"Jerrik," I commented. "She's an old woman."

"An old woman capable of taking you two out," she growled. "Now, what do you want with my grandson?"

Her...who now?

*Holy shit!* She *was* the Terminator's grandmother. "How is David your grandson? He's a werewolf, and well...you aren't."

"You think that matters?"

I caught her steely gaze and nodded. "Uh, yes?"

She cocked the gun and stared me down. "I won't ask again, dear."

For one brief moment, I debated telling her I intended to kill him. See how she reacted. But then that nasty gun of hers came back into focus and I realize it was a horrible idea. I'd been shot with silver before, not something I wanted to repeat.

"Look, we have a pack meeting today. An alpha from another pack is challenging my father. David wasn't there when my father announced the challenge. We're just trying to find him to ensure he doesn't miss it."

"Bullshit," she spat. "Doesn't take two of you for that."

Damn. Balls and brains. I kind of wished she was *my* grandmother.

Time to try a modicum of truth. "All right. Fine. I need him to testify. Your grandson isn't the little angel you think he is. He's a paid killer. Much like the wolf to my left here. David was hired to kill someone, and I need him to testify to that in front of both packs so we can avoid a war. Happy?"

She slid Jerrik a sideways glance, her cataract-infested eyes narrowing on him.

"And you? Why are you here?"

"Helping her," he snarled, jabbing a thumb in my direction.

"Are you going to kill him?"

"Wasn't planning on it," Jerrik responded.

Careful way of wording it. The only one here intending to kill David was me. Or maybe my father. Jerrik had nothing to do with that. So long as she didn't ask me...

She pondered our explanation, her wrinkled mouth pursed. A few more moments and her arms started to shake. I could sight down a gun for hours, but I had the muscle and toning and supernatural strength to assist me. The hunchback here had to be around ninety, and couldn't see for shit, let alone maintain a proper stance. Eventually, her arms started to lower.

"Fine," she murmured. "You'll find my David three blocks from here." She rattled off his address, then stepped back and slammed the door in our faces.

"Safe to say we're no longer welcome," I said.

Jerrik cupped my hand and lifted it to the light, his jaw tight as he studied the blisters. "They'll heal, but it'll take time."

"Mhm. Unfortunately, this is my sword hand."

He let loose a string of profanity, then glanced back

at the house as though considering breaking down the door and eating himself a grandmother. I didn't imagine she'd taste all that great, though.

"It's fine," I told him. "I've faced worse." But even I knew, this would slow my reaction times.

"Let's go. So long as she isn't lying, I know where we'll find David."

Twenty bucks said she'd lied. Somehow I felt like the Terminator's grandmother wouldn't give up that easily.

---

THE SECOND I stepped foot onto David's real street, I caught his scent. Funny how we'd spent a whole whopping five minutes together, but I'd memorized the bastard's aroma. Him having a knife to my throat had probably helped.

I glanced up at the smaller house before us and studied the exterior, silently wondering what booby-traps lay in store. I hadn't thought David the intelligent sort, but then again, I hadn't imagined his granny getting the drop on us. I honestly didn't know what to think anymore. Attacking me in broad daylight had screamed *idiot*, but had that been part of his plan? So many lingering questions.

"He's here," Jerrik confirmed, but like me, he didn't brave a step toward the house.

"Maybe we can call out to him? Tell him we know where his grandmother lives, and if he wants to see her again—"

The door swung open before I could finish my

sentence, and David filled the doorway. Definitely unexpected.

"What took you so long?" he said, leaning against the doorframe with his arms crossed over his chest. "Hurry up and get in here before someone sees you."

I shot a dubious glance around the neighborhood. Far as I could smell, we were the only ones out here. Even if they did see us, so what?

"Come on," he snapped, holding the door open wide. "You're letting the bugs in."

With a shrug, I started up his sidewalk with Jerrik hot on my trail. Only one way to find out if it was a trap. My body tightened with every step, prepared to defend myself if needed. But nothing happened. Huh. All right. I climbed the steps to David's porch and stopped right in of front him.

"What?" he asked.

"Just noticing how you look perfectly fine for a guy I stabbed with a silver blade."

"Does it matter?"

My head bobbed. "Hate wasting an attack like that. You could at least limp or something?"

He laughed under his breath and shook his head. "Hurry up and get inside. I want this conversation done as quickly as possible."

*Riiight.*

Jerrik placed a hand on my arm, halting me before I could cross the threshold. "What game are you playing?"

David rolled his eyes and gestured toward the back of his house. "Hurry up, will you?"

Clearly, we weren't going to get any answers out here. I stepped into his foyer and inspected our surroundings. From what I could see, nothing but walls and a rack of shoes. No hidden guns like granny three blocks over. But that didn't mean much. If he was anything like Jerrik, he probably lived a life full of paranoia. Which meant he'd have stashed a whole arsenal somewhere.

"Don't worry, Reagan, I have no interest in killing you anymore."

My narrowed eyes watched him stroll through the hallway to his living room. "Yeah? Why not?"

"Because the contract has been fulfilled, hasn't it? Word spread early this morning."

"Except, clearly you expected otherwise."

"Please. Doesn't matter what story you feed Benjamin about the two of you. I know what I saw. No way Jerrik would kill you. And I know where I stand." I moved to follow him, but he snapped his fingers in my direction. "Shoes. Please. Think we're all animals here?"

Was that an insult? I turned to Jerrik, laughter bubbling in my throat at the sight of him unlacing his massive combat boots. There was just something downright hilarious about seeing the shadow wolf walking through someone else's house in his white socked feet.

Chuckling under my breath, I followed suit and kicked off my joggers. A bungalow-style house, the hallway ran almost the entire length. It eventually widened into a massive kitchen with an attached dining room and an open living room fitted with massive bay windows that led out into a forest behind his house. It reminded me a bit of Jerrik's place, only smaller.

"Sit, please. I'll make us some coffee."

"None for me," Jerrik grunted, a sentiment I quickly echoed.

"It's not poisoned." David shook his head. "I said I had no interest in killing Reagan anymore, and I meant it."

"Yeah? How about explaining that change of heart," I interjected. "I would love to hear how a guy goes from bloodthirsty for a half a million to content with his lot in life."

David dragged a hand through his sandy-blonde hair and sat at the head of the table.

I couldn't resist—I checked beneath it for traps. Then ran my hand along the seam of the chair. Lord knew what I was looking for, I just knew I needed to check everything.

Both men watched me with identical amused expressions.

"You done?" David asked.

I gave a half-shrug, then sat down. Soft cushion, nice back support. I actually really liked his table. Could see myself getting a similar one for my place.

"Listen, maybe you're new to this, but generally once a contract has been filled, the job is done. Word spread around the infosphere that Jerrik had collected the fee."

*The infosphere. La dee dah.*

"So?"

"So, what do you expect me to do now? Say I did kill you. I could tell Benjamin it was all a ruse, sure. But

Jerrik has the money. And Lord knows where he stashed it. Something I doubt he'd ever tell me."

His upper lip curled back. "Not on your life."

"You can bet Benjamin won't cough up another half a million. Why would he? So, what point is there to me completing the job?"

"I did stab you," I pointed out, gesturing toward his side.

David shrugged. "Not the first time."

"Guess that sort of thing happens in your line of work."

A smug smile chased across Jerrik's face. "Not to me."

"Yes, yes, we all know you're the biggest, baddest wolf around."

He threw me a wink. "Damn right, dove."

We shared a grin, one that vanished when I turned back to David. "Why invite us in then?"

He sighed and dropped his hands down onto the table, his fingers twined loosely together. "Can we just skip all the formalities? And get down to business?"

"Oh, baby," I teased.

Jerrik shook his head. "Fine. You're compromised."

"I am."

My gaze leapt between the two of them. "Compromised?"

"You know his identity," Jerrik said. "If words gets out that he not only failed in his mission, but that the damn heir knows who he is, no one will ever hire him again. He invited us in because we aren't the only ones who want something here."

*Ohhh.* I liked that. Now I had grounds in which to convince him to help us. "How the tables have turned."

David shook his head. "Except, I know why *you're* here. And the two are counter-productive. Let me guess. You want me to testify in front of both packs that Benjamin hired me to assassinate you. If I do that, my cover's completely blown anyway. That's not what I want from you."

"It's not?" I asked.

"There's no way I'm remaining anonymous in all this. I should have turned down the bloody contract once I heard the shadow wolf took it. But half a million is a hell of a lot of money. I got greedy."

We agreed on that.

"Right now, I'll be lucky to escape with my life. Once Gabriel hears about all this…"

"You're dead," I finished. "That was sort of the plan."

David's gaze flicked to mine, his warm green eyes silently pleading with me. "I'll make you a deal. I'll testify in front of everyone, including your father. But afterward, I walk. I leave North America. You'll never hear from me again in your father's lifetime."

"Not good enough," I added.

His jaw tightened, disappointment curling his fingers into tight fists.

"This is how it's going to go down. My father isn't the one you assaulted. My father isn't the one you tried to kill. I am. He isn't the one you should be appeasing here. I'll make the deal with you and let you walk. But you're exiled for his lifetime, mine, and my children's."

His mouth fell open. "That could be like…"

"A couple thousand years. You won't be alive, that's for sure. But if somehow you are, those are my conditions. Take it, or we take you and head to the conclave, where you testify anyway, and then in front of everyone, I annihilate you."

"It's the best deal you're going to get," Jerrik assured him. "You fucked up."

Darkness whipped across David's face and he turned away as his wolf flared in his eyes. After a few moments, he finally nodded and glanced at me across the table. "Fine."

"Excellent. After everything is settled today, you'll have twenty-four hours to pack your things and arrange travel. Oh, and take your grandmother with you. That woman is..."

"Terrifying," Jerrik added in a mindless voice, as though he hadn't meant to speak the word aloud.

I nodded. In this case, we agreed.

"You want me to arrange travel for a ninety-year-old woman in twenty-four hours?"

"She seems capable," I said. "I have no fear she won't be able to handle it."

"She's human—you can't exile her."

"Can and just did. I'm sure she'll willingly leave when she learns it'll keep you alive."

David sighed and hung his head. After a few terse moments, he nodded, then raked his massive hands down his face. "Fine, agreed."

"It's settled then."

Jerrik leaned back in his chair and nodded.

I glanced down at my phone and grimaced when I

saw the time. Six fifty-five in the morning. Man, we were really pushing things. We had an hour and five minutes to get across the city. It would be close. Damn close.

"Fetch your best weapons," I said. "I refuse to let this challenge happen."

I would be the only person killing today.

I SAT in the front seat of Jerrik's truck, my fingers idly stroking Rory as he drove. Every few minutes, I shot the damn clock another glance, watching as the minutes ticked by. And with every passing second, my shoulders grew tighter. I didn't even care that David sat behind me, watching the sun pass through the clouds without a care in the world. To him, this challenge meant nothing. To me, it bordered on *everything*.

Seven forty-three. Seventeen minutes left until my entire world imploded. If we didn't make it in time, if they began the challenge...

I had to believe my father would win. I knew his strengths. He'd held the alpha position for over half a millennium. The thought of Benjamin winning today seemed ludicrous. Still, I couldn't help thinking that one day, he *would* be too old to stop a blade. And maybe today was that day. Benjamin had planned this down to the last detail. Gone so far as to "kill" me in an attempt to take over. What if his attempt worked? What if my death *did* affect my father?

This wasn't helping. I couldn't think like that.

"Distract me," I murmured to Jerrik, my nails clicking against my silver sword.

He stole a quick glance in my direction. "How?"

"I don't care," I whispered. "Talk to me. About anything. Just...distract me."

"All right. Tell me about your mother."

"Amalie?"

"Tell me why you always call them by their names," Jerrik urged.

I flattened my hand against Rory and sighed. "My father always thought it would help toughen me up if I didn't walk around calling for my *mama* or *papa*. Amalie hated it. She got this look every time I said her name. She'd scold my father and tell him I needed to be a girl a little while longer before he made me into a weapon, but Gabriel never listened. He'd always had this idea as to how he would raise his child. Eventually, she stopped arguing with him and just gave in." A faint smile chased across my face. "But whenever we were alone, I'd call her mama just to make her feel better. And I remember how she'd melt. She'd wrap her arms around me and whisper in my ear that no matter what Gabriel said or did, I would always be her little girl."

Tears pricked my eyes. Damn. I didn't realize how much she still affected my life.

"She died fifty-two years ago, while delivering another child."

"I didn't realize Gabriel has another kid."

"He doesn't," I whispered.

Jerrik reached out and took my hand, his thumb brushing over my knuckles.

"Not only was the child not his," I said, "but it also passed away."

"Gabriel didn't..." David murmured in the back.

"No, he didn't kill them. He and Amalie hadn't loved each other in a very long time. They both had their affairs. But he would never hurt her. It was just one of those tragic things."

I couldn't help it, I checked the time once more. Seven fifty-two.

My heart slammed into my ribs. Eight minutes left and we were still ten minutes away, minimum. I knew Gabriel. The fight would start on the hour without delay.

"Jerrik, drive faster. Please."

He put his foot down and accelerated without arguing. I only hoped the cops didn't pull us over. But if they did, I'd run the rest of the distance. I didn't care. Gabriel was hardly a perfect father, but he was the only one I had, and I refused to lose him.

"We'll make it in time," Jerrik assured me.

No, we wouldn't. If we hadn't taken the time to chase David down, we would have. But I couldn't labor on that thought. Not with Rory clutched in my hands. Not while I burned with the desire to run someone through.

"Jerrik?"

His fingers tightened around mine.

"After the fight..." I shouldn't be asking this question, but I had to know. "No matter the outcome, are you planning on leaving?"

A few tense moments passed before he released my hand and held the steering wheel instead. "I don't know."

*I don't know* was better than *yes*, but still his answer burned. I wanted him to stay. I wanted more from him. But I understood his dilemma. My father would never accept him as part of the pack. I'd seen Jerrik's strength, and I knew my father. The two would clash and it'd result in another challenge.

"Let's not think about that now," he said. "Focus on the challenge and Benjamin. We can talk after."

A light chuckle rose from the back seat. "Never thought I'd see the day."

I didn't reach back and throttle him, but damn, I was tempted.

"The shadow wolf in love."

I sucked in a sharp breath and snuck a peek at Jerrik. His white-knuckled grip tightened on the steering wheel and his jaw looked tight enough to shatter. That he didn't deny David's statement made my heart skip an entire beat.

"We'll talk about this after," he said.

I nodded. We definitely would. Until then, I leaned my head back against the chair and closed my eyes while counting my breaths. Staring at the clock wouldn't help matters. We'd either make it or we wouldn't. I had to focus on the things I could control.

With every breath, I centered my thoughts and focused on preparation. I'd borrowed a few of David's weapons, and I took a silent inventory as the car sped through the city. Dagger strapped to my thigh, check. Rory in my hands, check. Two wrist sheaths with throwing knives, check. And for emergency purposes, a sleek Barretta tucked against the small of my back. The packs generally used silver blades for their fights—carried over from the good ol' days. But I refused to run headlong into a gun fight with only a sword.

The car turned and I snapped open my eyes. My father's estate filled my vision—a massive, vintage mansion that sat on the edge of town. Gabriel loved his space, and had purchased the surrounding thousand acres of land. In other words, no one around for miles to hear the fight.

Jerrik squealed to a stop in front of the countless other cars and slammed the car into park.

Seven fifty-eight. We'd made it. But now, we needed to find my father. Without hesitation, I shoved open my door and climbed out. Rory's scabbard rested against my back, but I held him in my hands, just in case. My father had always used the oversized backyard to fight his battles. Less to break and more space to maneuver. From the sight of the teeming crowd gathered around the side of the house, it seemed the challenge was about to begin.

*Screw that.*

I bolted toward the house, ignoring Jerrik's calls behind me. Sorry boys, but my father was the last of my family. I refused to stand around and wait for them.

The second I reached the crowd, three of Benjamin's wolves turned toward me, their mouths dropping open.

"You're supposed to be dead."

"Sorry to disappoint," I growled, knowing they'd hear me over the din. "Move."

They shared a glance, then flexed their hands—claws like scythes sprouting from their fingers.

I lifted a brow. "Seriously?"

"You're supposed to be dead," the first repeated. "If Benjamin hears that we let you through…"

*Jesus.* Was the whole pack in on his scheme? Maybe I shouldn't have bothered trying to prevent a war.

"You're gonna wanna rethink this," I snapped. "Attack me, you die. Let me pass, and maybe Gabriel will give you enough time to run back home before we hunt you down like the traitors you are."

"Traitors." The second wolf shook his head. "We're loyal to our alpha."

"To Christian?" I demanded.

The third spat on the ground. "He ain't our alpha."

A coup then. Which made me wonder how many here were loyal to Benjamin, and how many to Christian. It also made me wonder if Christian was even still alive.

The sound of my father's deafening snarl rent the morning air. My pulse quickened—I needed to reach him, needed to assure him that I was alive.

Which meant cleaving my way through these asshats and whoever else wanted to stand in my way. I leaned forward and unleashed my alpha stare. "You really don't want to test me."

The first and third shared a grin. "I think we do."

I stepped back and held out my arms. "Don't say I didn't warn you."

One of the wolves leapt forward. I didn't stop to see

*My Viking Wolf*

which. His claws sliced at the air near my throat, but I feinted back. A typical attack. Everyone went for the throat. The belly was next, and I dodged to the left, leading him away from his two friends. As a default, all werewolves were dangerous. But my father had spent the past ninety years training me to fight. With a small smile, I stepped to the side when he lunged, grabbed him by the back of the neck and buried Rory through his chest, piercing his heart in one swift move.

Somehow above the din, I caught the sound of his startled gasp. Before he could fall, I yanked Rory free and spun, cleaving my blade through the next clawed hand that swiped in my direction. The werewolf howled and staggered back, clutching at his bleeding stump. Thankfully, Jerrik stuck his own blade through the werewolf's open mouth, ending his cries before they attracted the rest of the crowd.

"Oh, didn't see you there," I commented.

"Yeah, I noticed. You've got some blood on you." He pointed at my face.

I shrugged. Probably wouldn't be the only blood on me before the end of the morning.

"Jesus," the third werewolf whispered, stumbling backward.

Others turned toward us, the scent of blood drawing their attention. They turned one-by-one, their eyes glowing. Fighting really did bring out the worst in us. I debated shifting. But if I shifted, I'd lose the ability to speak and reason with people. I didn't want to kill *everyone*.

"Well?" David asked, appearing on my left.

"We do what we have to," I said. The sound of my father's battle waged on, and the fact that he hadn't yet put Benjamin down worried me. "I need to get up there. Can you two handle this?"

Though Benjamin's people surrounded us, it was the familiar faces in the crowd that I looked to. My packmates stared back at me with identical shocked expressions.

"Yes, I'm alive," I called out. "And I *need* to speak to my father. But Benjamin's pack won't let me pass."

A steady thrum of growls broke through the crowd, my own people rising to the occasion. Bodies began to shift everywhere, the sound of clothing tearing open. The massacre I'd hoped to avoid seemed inevitable now. Who knew how deep this coup went? But that wasn't my job to sort out.

"Stand aside," I said, before pointing down at their two dead wolves. "Or join them."

The crowd moved as one, and from every direction, my loyal wolves poured toward me, drawing an invisible line in the proverbial sand. Benjamin's wolves weren't sure how to respond, their anxious gazes darting to me. Christian was nowhere in sight. So either, Benjamin had already killed his father, or he somehow remained oblivious as to his son's actions.

I studied the many faces staring back at me. They didn't encompass the entirety of the wolves Benjamin had brought to our country, but close. In fact, almost equal to the number of my wolves now standing at my back. Had they limited the number of people allowed to attend the challenge? My father had done so in the past.

When Benjamin's wolves didn't move, I nodded and spun Rory, flicking the blood off my blade. "This is your last warning. Stand down."

I caught sight of my father, a towering inferno of a beast lumbering backward. Injured. I didn't have *time* for this.

"Screw it. I'm going through you, even if that means cutting each of you down."

I took a step forward, spinning Rory in my hand for dramatic effect. One of Benjamin's wolves darted toward me, but before he closed the distance, I grabbed one of the daggers in my wrist sheath and let it fly. It slid through my challenger's eye like butter and dropped him in two seconds flat.

Silence spread through the remainder of Benjamin's wolves. They didn't look so confident anymore. So I shoved through them, and kicked down the next one who stood in my path. The solid boot to his gut drove him to the ground, where his own people held him down.

"Let her pass," they started to murmur amongst themselves.

Wise decision.

The moment I made it to the clearing, my heart leapt into my throat. Benjamin actually had the upper hand. My father stumbled to the side, blood gushing from a series of wounds sliced into his sides. Practically eviscerated. I needed to *stop* this, but the two were lost to their bloodlust.

Gabriel straightened, and swiped at Benjamin's throat, catching chunks of flesh. With a deafening snarl, he lunged forward, his teeth bared. For a moment, it looked as though Gabriel would win, but Benjamin feinted to the side at the last moment and caught Gabriel's other side with his claws.

Gabriel toppled over, his legs sliding out beneath him. Benjamin rose, a towering tawny-colored wolf, and rushed forward for the kill.

"No!" I screamed.

Time slowed the second I darted into the fight. Distantly, I heard Jerrik yell my name, I heard the howls of my pack, but I could only see my father, helpless and injured, his eyes defeated. He *knew* he would die here. I refused to let that happen.

I rushed between the two massive werewolves and dropped to my knees. I slid on the ground beneath Benjamin and slashed with my blade. A hot splash of blood sprayed my face. Not enough to kill Benjamin but enough to get his attention.

Darting back to my feet, I turned and faced him, Rory clutched between my hands. His eyes shot wide at the sight of me, his lips reared back.

"Surprised?" I mocked, hoping to keep his attention on me and away from Gabriel. "Come on, big boy. I'm the one you want, right? But instead of challenging me, you hired assassins."

Gabriel picked himself up with a loud snarl, his furious gaze burning a hole through Benjamin. A little of his old fire flared in his eyes as he stepped toward me.

"This challenge between Gabriel and Benjamin is unsanctioned!" I shouted to everyone listening. "Your packmate, and my so-called fiancé put a hit out on my life! His goal was to kill me, so that when he challenged Gabriel, he'd be emotionally compromised."

"It's true," David spoke up, fulfilling our end of the agreement. "When the first assassin failed in his task, Benjamin sent me to finish the job. I stand here before you because Reagan allowed me to live when she could have killed me. I promised to testify before both packs."

"And for those who need further proof, we have photos and a recording of Benjamin speaking with one of the assassins he hired." I could have mentioned Jerrik, but I wanted to keep his name out of this. I knew I'd need to tell my father, but the pack didn't need to know who he was. Not yet.

Gabriel's claws dug into the earth as he limped toward me. To say he was pissed would be an understatement. He looked like a demon, eyes blazing and lips reared back over his monstrous fangs. He stood next to me, a mountainous wolf, his head nearly reaching my shoulders.

"Perhaps you should all ask yourself if this is the alpha you want! If Christian is too weak to hold or control your pack, handle it as *real* werewolves. Find someone better suited than this scheming coward who put out a hit on his fiancée to take over an entire pack."

Benjamin snarled, his head dropping low. I saw his intentions clear as day and gripped Rory tight. There wasn't enough time to shift to compensate. And I refused to let Gabriel take this blow.

Without warning, Benjamin lunged, his lethal claws extended. I sucked in a breath, my gaze narrowing on his throat when an enormous black wolf leapt into the fray.

*Jerrik.* He smashed into Benjamin's side and the two spilled to the ground, snapping and biting at each other. Jerrik came out on top and raked his claws down Benjamin's chest, splitting him from neck to navel. Benjamin howled in agony, but still darted to his feet. Jerrik lunged forward and ripped off a chunk of his shoulder with one brutal bite, then threw him like a rag doll across the yard.

I released the breath I hadn't realized I was holding and strode toward Benjamin and Jerrik, my father at my side. I twined my fingers through Jerrik's fur, content when I saw him uninjured. The same couldn't be said for Benjamin who lay moaning on the grass. Sinew, flesh, and fur rolled over his shoulder in an attempt to heal the injury. We werewolves were tough bastards. If I walked away, Benjamin would heal the gaping wound, but I refused to let that happen.

"Watch out," I told Jerrik.

He stepped back, his muzzle slick with blood. There, in front of every last one of Benjamin's loyal wolves, I raised Rory above my head and brought him down on Benjamin's neck, severing his head from the rest of his body. It rolled off into the grass, the fur melting away from his face until his human half was all that remained.

Not that it mattered.

Benjamin was dead. And with his death came an eerie silence.

# 15

WEREWOLVES as far as the eye could see. Everywhere I looked, another familiar face stared back.

"Reagan," Lucy laughed as she forced her way through the crowd. She threw her arms around my neck and dragged me in for a bone-crushing hug. "Girl, never pull that shit again."

"I hope I'll never have to," I said while patting her back. It felt damn good to be surrounded by my pack again.

"Gabriel is gonna want to talk to you. So, I'll wait for you outside, sound good?"

"You sure? It might be awhile."

A shadow whisked across her face and she shot a sly glance toward Jerrik. "Yeah, I'll wait for you."

Appreciation had my arms tightening around her. God, what would I do without this woman in my life?

She knew today might end disastrously for me, but she was here for me no matter what. Hell, the whole pack could probably sense my nerves. Killing Benjamin had been the easy part compared to what lay ahead.

"All of you. Out."

I lifted my head at the sound of my father's gruff voice, my pulse thundering in my head. Here came the moment of truth. Gabriel wasn't in any position to challenge Jerrik. But I knew my father. That wouldn't stop him from trying.

Quite a few stopped to pat me on the back and shoot Jerrik a curious glance before filing out the back door and into their cars.

"Not you," my father growled when David started for the door.

Even I caught David's wince before he turned and slunk back into the house.

Eventually Jerrik, David, Gabriel, and I were all that remained. With space to move around, Jerrik crossed the room and stood next to me, our hands brushing. My father's eyes zeroed in on the gesture, his jaw tightening.

Still, he chose not to question us. Instead, he limped toward me and held out his arms. Gabriel was a tough son of a bitch, but in private, he'd always shown me the love and adoration a father reserved for his daughter.

With a watery laugh, I walked into his arms and sank into the embrace. "I almost didn't make it in time."

"I'm fine, honey. I'm just so relieved to see you alive. Yesterday..." He shuddered. "I never want to think about that day again."

I'd heard some talk already, but the most telling

evidence was the demolished state of my father's house. Picture frames torn from the clawed-up walls, the dining room table shattered into pieces...the place was a downright mess.

"You're going to need to call a designer I think."

Even he laughed. "The house needs a remodeling anyway."

Sure. We could pretend that.

"All right, baby girl. Let's start from the top."

And so I did. I started with the club and launched into meeting Jerrik, though I kept the conversation PG. My father didn't need to hear about the night we spent together. By the time I'd finished, my father had moved to the couch and now sat with his head clutched between his hands. I knew he had to be tired. Otherwise he never would have sat in front of Jerrik and David while they stood.

"I understand why you did what you did," he said. "I just wish you would have come to me first."

"I was trying to prevent a war. I knew if we killed Benjamin without proof, things would descend into chaos."

"Christian's alive, thankfully. I received a call after the healer finished bandaging me—one of his wolves found him in his hotel room, unconscious. Benjamin tried to kill him but failed."

I nodded, relieved. "At least they still have their alpha."

"And I'm still alive, as is our entire pack. I'm grateful for what you did. I just wish it hadn't come to all this."

I sat down next to Gabriel and rested my head on his shoulder. "Me too. I'm just glad you're alive."

Gabriel patted my knee, then lifted his gaze and stared at David. "And you?"

David snapped to attention, a little fear dancing in his eyes.

"I believe my daughter gave you twenty-four hours to get the hell out. Might want to get started on that."

"Yes, sir," David mumbled. Without another word, he turned and ducked through the back door, vanishing from sight.

"I don't think we'll see him again. Not in his lifetime, anyway."

That sounded ominous. "Gabriel..."

"Don't worry. I'll give him a head start."

"No. I swore to him. He could have fought me or escaped during all the chaos, he didn't. Promise me you'll keep my end of the bargain."

My father sighed but eventually nodded. "Fine. The things I do for you."

"Right, about that..."

He leaned back and laughed softly. "You know, of all the reckless things I expected of you, this is by far the worst. You know who he is?"

I rolled my eyes. "Of course I know who he is. The question is, do you?"

"Sweetheart, you don't forget the ones who nearly kill you. Much like I'll never forget Benjamin, I'll never forget the shadow wolf."

Well, they hadn't tried to kill each other yet. That was something, right? Course, Jerrik also hadn't spoken yet. Who knew the thoughts churning in that head of his? He leaned against the wall across from us, his expression fathomless.

My father rested his hands against his thighs and pushed to his feet, a little slower than normal. "Tell me, boy. Do *you* remember when last we met?"

*Boy*. Jerrik had centuries on him. Sometimes Gabriel astounded me.

A taunting smile chased across Jerrik's lips. "You don't forget the men you *almost* kill."

Wow. "Was that really necessary?"

"It's fine," my father commented aimlessly. "You know, when you and I first met, I never would have imagined this moment. I always thought you'd come sniffing around the pack, and when that day came, I honestly suspected I'd have to hand the pack over to you. But not my daughter."

"I don't want your pack," Jerrik said.

"But you *do* want Reagan."

My heartbeat sped up. "Gabriel—"

He held up a hand. "No. This answer must come from him."

"Does it matter?" Jerrik grumbled.

"It does to me," Gabriel said.

And it did to me. But I refused to force him into this answer. No one liked being put on the spot like that. "Gabriel, just let him—"

A sharp growl silenced me. I sighed and dropped my head into my palms. Jerrik and I had known each other for a few days, nothing more. Granted, those days felt like a lifetime right now, but that didn't mean he was ready to answer such a question. Nor was I ready to hear the answer. Trust Gabriel to force our hands.

"It *doesn't* matter what I want," Jerrik snapped. "I know *you*, Gabriel. I know how you think, how you operate. I've seen you at your worst, which is generally the moment people show their true faces. You would never let me join your pack, and I refuse to take Reagan's last living parent from her."

*Wait, what?*

I slowly lifted my head and stared at Jerrik. He caught my gaze and offered a sad smile. "I've wanted you since the moment I saw you in the bar. I've heard other werewolves talk about finding their mates and how they *knew* the moment they met. That moment hit me the second I stepped into that bar and caught your scent." He pushed off the wall and crouched in front of me, taking my hands in his. "When I first saw you, my entire world flipped. I knew right then and there. But I also knew nothing permanent would come of us because your father would challenge me the second he laid eyes on me. I have no place in your pack. And I won't take your father from you. I would never do that to you."

Tears pricked my eyes. So that was why he'd hesitated whenever I'd asked if he'd stay. "I knew the second you bought me that shot," I said with a watery laugh.

He cupped my face, then leaned forward and brushed a kiss across my brow. I bit back a sob. It felt like he was saying goodbye, and I wasn't ready for that.

"Has anyone thought to ask me what *I* think about all this?" Gabriel asked.

I knuckled a few sneaky tears away from my cheeks and glanced at him. "We all know what you think."

"Clearly not. I think you two are perfect for each other."

I froze, my eyes narrowing on my father. Had Benjamin knocked something loose in his head? Rattled that brain of his around a little too hard?

He caught my expression and chuckled. "You look so much like your mother when you glare at me like that. Sometimes I forget what it's like to care for someone. And you're hardly a child anymore. I knew the moment Jerrik dove into the fight to protect you from Benjamin that he felt something real for you. So, here's my offer."

An offer? What? I'd never known Gabriel to make a concession for anyone. Those who stood in his way, he killed. He'd taken over the pack and led them to a new world, and no one had ever come close to taking it from him. Until today.

"Jerrik may join our pack. The shadow wolf may not."

"I don't understand." Weren't they the same person?

"As it stands, no one knows the shadow wolf's real identity. I will allow Jerrik to join our pack on the condition that he find himself a new day job. And that no one in the pack learn of his *other* identity."

I blinked at my father. Was he serious? He couldn't be. Gabriel didn't understand how to compromise. He never had. Not with my mother. Not with *anyone*.

He walked toward me and held out his hands. I slid my fingers over his palms and stood.

"Consider this my gift to you. When I thought you

were dead, I would have given anything to have you back. If Jerrik truly has no intentions of challenging *me*, then I can agree to do the same. But the shadow wolf dies." He glanced behind me. "Give me your word. I won't have my daughter mated to some lowlife assassin."

"You have my word," Jerrik said without hesitation.

My head spun. Of all the scenarios I'd imagined, this hadn't even crossed my mind. The darkest part of my brain had pictured them tearing into one another, as alpha werewolves often did. This was unprecedented.

"The pack will sense Jerrik is stronger than you," I said. "Can you live with that?"

"They'll see that we came to an agreement. I'm serious, though. No one hears that he's the shadow wolf. Understood?"

I nodded, completely flabbergasted.

"I'll leave you two be now. I'm sure you have some things to discuss." Gabriel dragged me into his chest for another suffocating hug, then left out the back door.

I stood there, my mind blank. I had no clue how to respond.

Jerrik's hand brushed mine and I turned toward him. "I..." I shook my head, at a loss for words. "I really don't know what just happened."

He grinned at me and cupped my face. "Do you want to be with me? Just me?"

"Are you kidding me?"

He shook his head.

"Of course I do."

"My past doesn't bother you? What I did, who I am?"

This time, I shook my head. I understood his reasons

now that I knew more of his past. Hard to blame him for killing what he thought were monsters. "We both have our pasts. It's our future I care about. But are you okay with giving up who you are? Walking away from the shadow wolf?"

"He died the second I saw you in that club," he said. Without another word, he swooped down and claimed my mouth in a soul searing kiss. When we broke apart, he leaned back and smoothed my hair away from my cheeks. "This is it then, I'm yours."

"And I'm yours."

"Forever."

I stretched up onto my tiptoes and kissed him again. "Forever and always, my Viking wolf."

# EPILOGUE

**Two months later**

THE FIRST SNOWFALL blanketed Jerrik's backyard, the trees dusted with white. Quite a beautiful sight. In the city, winter came in a disgusting mess of sloppy roads and icy sidewalks. But out here, I could enjoy the view.

I sat in one of his patio chairs, bundled up in a thick blanket. Catsanova sat in my lap, purring up a storm, his eyes half-closed as I stroked his chin. In the two months since we'd met, he'd become my constant companion. Much like Jerrik. We'd barely stepped foot outside his house, enjoying the peace and quiet.

Gabriel had even made an effort to come visit. It'd been tense as all hell, but they'd muddled their way through it. Every now and then I'd caught the tightening of jaws and flashing of eyes, but they'd restrained themselves for my sake. And I'd shown my appreciation by baking them a couple dozen delicious cookies that they'd devoured in record time.

I had hope. One day, their status would no longer matter.

Heavy footsteps echoed through the house—the telltale sound of Jerrik's combat boots. I listened as the back patio door slid open, and smiled when he laid his arm against the back of my seat.

I tipped my head back and met his gaze. "Hi."

He leaned down and kissed me, lingering for a moment before taking his own seat at my side.

"Where've you been?" I asked.

"Talking with Gabriel, believe it or not."

Catsanova read the sudden tension in my body, his eyes popping open as he mewled at me.

"Don't worry, dove," Jerrik said with a light laugh. "We worked something out."

"Okay..."

"He's created a new position in the pack for me."

*Oh, God.* I couldn't say why, but the image of Jerrik dressed up as a jester darted through my head.

"Nothing so bad as what you're thinking," Jerrik chuckled. "He wants to create a spy network. To ensure that what happened with Benjamin never happens again. I have connections, more than even he knows about. So, he wants me to head up this new division."

Relief loosened my muscles and Catsanova settled back in, kneading my lap.

Jerrik shot him a glance, his mouth curving upward. "Traitor."

"Hey, you said he was a lady-killer. He's only proving

you right." I scratched behind Catsanova's ears and was rewarded with a long, contented purr. "So, this is a good thing, right? This job?"

"Well, I already have enough money to live a couple dozen lifetimes, but it'll give your father and I a chance to work together. Maybe come to an understanding. The wolf in him doesn't believe I have no interest in taking over the pack. It's an instinct thing."

I nodded. I knew how that worked.

"I think it'll be good," Jerrik announced, his focus straying out into the trees. "It's beautiful out here."

I hummed and leaned back in the chair, my head resting against his arm. "I like it here."

"Really? It's not too far away from Gabriel or Lucy?"

My eyes slipped close as I shook my head. "It's just perfect. So serene. I feel like I can just be me here, you know? Not the heir. Just Reagan."

"Good." Jerrik shifted his position, his fingers twining with mine.

Yes, I could definitely spend the rest of my life right here and never worry about anything ever again. I leaned over and rested my head against his shoulder, breathing in his familiar scent.

Jerrik slid something on my finger.

My eyes popped open and I stared down at my hand, my heart screeching to a dead stop at the sight of my mother's engagement ring sparkling up at me. "Jerrik...what..."

He slid off his chair and knelt before me, his hands gripping mine. "Reagan, before I met you, I knew only misery. I was trapped in this endless cycle of torment and loneliness. I thought I'd been cursed by my gods. But then I saw you. I knew right then and there that you were meant for me. Before you, I was nothing more than the shadow wolf. And then you swept into my life and burned away all the darkness. For the first time in countless centuries, I feel alive. I feel loved. And I'm happy. If you'll let me, I'll spend the rest of my life making you feel the same way."

"Jerrik..."

"I told Gabriel this was my intention. And he gave me this ring to give to you. He said it was the ring he gave your mother."

I nodded, my pulse thundering in my ears. This was the last thing I'd expected when waking this morning. And now, I could barely find the words.

"I want to marry you, dove," Jerrik said. "And your father gave his blessing."

A watery laughed spilled from my lips. I pushed Catsanova aside and lunged toward Jerrik, wrapping my arms around his neck. "I wouldn't have cared if he'd said no."

Jerrik drew back. "So, that's a yes?"

"Of course it's a yes."

The tears I'd been fighting against slipped down my cheeks. And for the first time ever, I didn't care. Jerrik grinned at me, his face igniting with true happiness. He brushed away my tears, then leaned in and kissed me.

Excitement bubbled within me. I broke from the kiss and leaned back, still laughing at the sight of my mother's ring on my finger. So beautiful, the way it sparkled in the winter sunlight.

*My Viking Wolf*

"I need to tell Lucy," I babbled. "She'll be so excited! Another bachelorette party."

Jerrik laughed. "Just no cakes this time."

"I'm thinking strippers," I teased.

Growling playfully, Jerrik sat back in his chair.

I picked up my phone and turned on the screen. "Oh, she just texted me a few moments ago. A picture of something. I can't make out what that is. The sun is too bright."

Jerrik leaned over and cupped a hand over the top of the phone, casting a shadow over the screen. The picture came into focus and we both sucked in a sharp breath at the same time.

Lucy had sent me a photo, all right. My eyes narrowed in on the two pink lines. Beneath it, she'd written: *So, I'm pregnant.*

I shot Jerrik a stunned stare. "Holy shit."

Guess today was full of surprises.

# WHISPERS IN THE DARK EXCERPT

NOT AGAIN...

Madison White pinched the bridge of her nose and released a long breath. This wasn't happening. She had to be trapped in some hell dimension where she'd been put in charge of her demon cub sister—the only possible explanation, really. Because her baby sister *knew* better than to pull this shit again, especially considering they'd just had a chat about this yesterday.

Apparently not, though, because there it was. Blood, torn feathers, ragged flesh dangling from the beast's gnawed bones... And the little punk hadn't thought to bury the massacred beast. Oh no, she'd dragged the mutilated carcass into their friggin' house and displayed it like a prize on Maddie's goose down pillow.

Worse! Her stomach actually growled as though the half-mangled corpse were appetizing.

*No.* A snarl vibrated within the deepest pit of Maddie's chest. Inwardly, she swatted her wretched cat on the nose and forced her back into the quietest recess of her mind. *Focus.* She would not encourage such behavior. Being half-animal hardly meant she could go through life acting like one. When she stood on two legs, she was human, and she bloody well intended to behave accordingly. Humans did *not* leap onto a bed and bat around a dead bird. They just didn't, no matter how badly her mountain lioness wanted out to play.

"Paige!" Her youngest sister's name spilled from her downturned lips in a yowling shriek. "Get your fuzzy little ass in here right now!"

Because it *had* to have been her. No one else in this house would have trounced a friggin' hawk and left it as a gift on her pillow. Yesterday, it'd been a half-eaten gopher draped across their kitchen counter. Their cook had nearly suffered an embolism when she'd come across the dismembered creature. Madison had struggled to provide an explanation. Her pitiful *girls will be girls* excuse hadn't cut it, and now they were short one cook. Seemed her baby sister took great joy in playing whack-a-mole out in the fields, but that didn't forgive the behavior.

Which, all right, after the past three weeks, seeing her sister take joy in *anything* was a relief. But that hardly meant the little brat could drag the remains of her play toys into the house. A whole world of *hell no.*

"Paige!" Maddie spun on her heel in time to catch sight of a fully shifted cougar cub darting into the nearest bedroom. A deep growl scraped past Maddie's curled lips. "I'm not playing with you, kid. Get in here, right now."

A soft wheeze rose to Maddie's ears, the distinct

sound of a laughing feline. Lord save her from little children. *She's ten*, Maddie reminded herself. At that age, she'd been a hellion too, a real handful for her parents. But never—*never*—had she taunted them with dead animals. Their father would have tanned her already tan backside.

"Paige."

She sucked in a deep breath and counted to ten. Repeatedly. This was her job now. She had to play the role of the calm and collected guardian as opposed to the indignant sister. Had to teach her siblings this sort of conduct was inappropriate—shifter or not. So no, she couldn't go chasing after Paige, no matter how badly her cat wanted to. If she gave in to *that* side of herself, there was no telling what sort of chaos the house would descend into. With their father's death so fresh, she had to keep hold of herself and had to show her sisters she was a responsible adult.

"Paige. Get out here. Now. Don't make me start counting." Though she hadn't a clue what she would do if her sister called her bluff. No one had ever been stupid enough to ignore their father. When he'd yowled, they'd come running. So far, her demands had only been met with giggles.

A great start to her new role as guardian.

Seemed luck was on her side today, though. Perhaps Paige sensed her frustrated tone or knew that this was not the time to upset her further. Either way, she popped her head out the door, her playful grin slipping at the sight of Maddie's face. Her sister was a right mess, her fluffy fur muddied and knotted, her spotted sides barely visible beneath all the dirt and blood. Not to mention, she reeked of horses, cattle, and carrion. The joys of living on a ranch.

Sighing, Maddie raked a hand through her own hair. How the hell was she supposed to handle this? It hadn't been a month yet since their father's death, and Paige had only begun to bounce back. Yesterday was the first time Maddie had seen her in cougar form since the funeral. Scolding her felt wrong, but she had to set boundaries. She couldn't allow either of her sisters to run rampant.

Brooklyn had never given her this sort of trouble. Of course, she was also seven years older than Paige. And nine years younger than Maddie. When Brooklyn had been learning to shift, Maddie had been out helping her father in the fields. Now, at seventeen, Brooklyn came with her own set of problems, ones that downright terrified Maddie. The thought of getting her sister through prom and boys and sex made her shudder.

A cold nose pressed against her palm, startling Maddie out of her thoughts. *Right*. Dead animal. Shifted sister. She needed to handle this.

Maddie released another long breath before crouching down to her baby sister's level. She took her scruffy cheeks between her hands and held her face still. "You have ten minutes to shift back, get dressed, and clean my room. Do you understand me?"

Her sister's hot tongue scraped against her hand.

"I mean it, Paige." Today was not the day for this. Two of her father's associates intended to drop by today to discuss some concerns. Always something, it seemed, and she doubted that would change anytime soon.

Her days had once been simple. Riding in the fields with the men, tending to the cattle and grain. Now, everyone expected her to sit behind the big desk and maintain the entire estate. She'd always known her father would leave White Ranch to her, but she'd never dreamed it would happen at the ripe age of twenty-six.

The feel of her sister's fur shifting against her palms drew her attention, and Maddie watched as the cougar melted away, leaving behind a sweet little girl with a filthy face.

"Clean this up?" Maddie asked.

Paige nodded. "I'm sorry."

Maddie leaned forward and brushed a light kiss against the tip of her sister's nose. "I know you are. Just get washed up. We'll have company any minute now."

Her sister turned and bolted toward the bathroom, her grubby fingers marring the clean walls. Maddie tipped her head back, and once again found herself asking for a little help. Managing the girls had been different—*easier*—when their father was alive. It had felt simpler, somehow, with the two of them tag-teaming them. Now, all the responsibility rested on her shoulders, and she wasn't sure she could handle it. Overnight she'd become a single parent.

"Knock, knock!" a baritone voice shouted from across the house.

Maddie cursed under her breath, then stepped into the hall and wrenched her bedroom door shut behind her. Both of her father's associates were shifters—they would undoubtedly pick up on the dead bird's scent. Not much she could do about that.

"Anyone home?"

"Come in," Maddie called out.

She knew the voice. It belonged to her father's lawyer, Scott Delaney. Maddie shuddered when his sharp aroma invaded her house. She drew in a breath and shook her head. Nine years, and still the scent of werewolf evoked a visceral response deep in her gut. Every bone in her body ached to tear him to shreds, but she tamped it back. Her father had never understood her distaste for the wolfier kind. But even though the ranch was in her name now, she had no intention of replacing Mr. Delaney. He'd worked with her father for years. The issue was hers, and after close to a decade, it seemed about time she worked through it.

Of course, it didn't help that they lived right outside a city *full* of the wretched beasts. Hell, they'd even named the place after them: *Wolffe Peak*.

Heavy footsteps echoed in the foyer. Maddie glanced over her to shoulder to ensure her bedroom door was shut, then started toward the kitchen. The fewer people who approached her room, the better. At least until she cleaned up her sister's mess...and possibly fumigated.

"Mornin'," Scott rumbled the moment she came into sight.

With a weak smile, Maddie gestured toward the kitchen table. "Hello, Mr. Delaney. Coffee?"

His nose wrinkled, and her breath caught. He was a werewolf, surely he understood the hassle of raising a cub. "Might I suggest something a bit stronger. Like bleach?"

Her shoulders slumped. "Is it that bad?"

A light laugh fell from his lips. "My son keeps me on my toes. Believe me, I'm no stranger to the smell of dead animal."

For the first time ever, Maddie cracked a smile at the werewolf. "I never pulled anything like this when I was young."

"Good for you." He tapped his briefcase, then popped it open and retrieved a thick folder. "Now, let's get this sorted quickly so you can clean that up. In here is everything your father had laid out in the event of his death."

She cringed at the blunt statement. It'd been three weeks since her father had passed, and the pain wasn't as fresh now, but it still stung.

"I'll need you to look this over and sign some papers for me. Just general things, like transferring the ranch and land all to your name."

Maddie blinked. "Just me? He didn't leave anything to Brooklyn or Paige?"

"Paige is ten," Scott reminded her. "And Brooklyn... well, your daddy knew who best fit the ranch. Now, that isn't to say he didn't take care of them. They both have a home here for their rest of their lives or until you sell, and both have a very substantial inheritance ready for them when they reach the right age, but the primary business and properties will be listed under your name."

Nodding, Maddie's gaze dropped to the briefcase. Inside was the sum of her father's pride and joy...the deed to the ranch. Even though it was little more than a slip of paper, she felt the weight of responsibility settle on her shoulders. Her parents had poured every ounce of themselves into White Ranch. It'd been more than a business to them—it'd been their home. And now that they were both gone, it was up to her to ensure it thrived.

She ran her fingers down the folder. "I'll take good care of it."

"Now, hold on there," Scott interjected. "You aren't the sole owner of White Ranch."

Maddie froze, her gaze narrowing on the werewolf. "What? Who else is there?" She and her sisters were the last of the family. Their mother had died during Paige's birth, their grandparents long before that, and her father had been an only child. There wasn't anyone else left.

Scott flipped open the folder and tapped a fresh sheet of paper. Skim-reading, her mouth gaped, her insides burning when she caught sight of the breakdown.

Dean Brewington, she could understand. He'd been her father's silent business partner for years. Handing him ten percent made complete sense.

But— "Axel Galliard?" His name fell from her lips in a fevered shout. "Are you freaking kidding me?"

She snatched up the papers and held them to the light, as though searching for a misprint or some sort of stupid joke. Unfortunately, Axel's name *had* been scratched into the pristine paper, the familiar swirls of her father's handwriting doing nothing to settle her now seething blood pressure.

She continued to read, a threatening growl rumbling deep in her chest when she saw his allotted portion. "Twenty-five percent?" she howled. Maddie slapped the sheet down on the table and shoved to her feet. This was ridiculous! Why the hell would her father give *him* anything?

"Maddie?" Scott leaned forward and read over the sheet.

"He was a foreman," she sputtered. "Nothing more than that. He...he..." She raked a ruthless hand through her hair and scrunched up her nose in thought. *He* was also the reason she hated werewolves. What the hell had her father been thinking? She spun on her heel, pinning Scott with a severe glare. "Does he know yet?"

"Uh, no." Scott cleared his throat, clearly stunned by her reaction. "I'd thought I'd leave that to you."

Her eyes slipped closed. This was a nightmare. What had her father done? And why? There was no logic to it. She hadn't seen Axel in nine years, not since... *No.* She forced that memory aside. Now wasn't the time to relive her girlish fantasies. Or nightmares, as it were.

Why would her father do this? Write a man they barely knew into his will, a man who'd shown no loyalty to her or the ranch. Anger churned in the pit of her stomach. Axel must have done *something* to leverage her father.

Trembling, she met Scott's gaze once more. "I don't even know where he lives anymore." Nor did she want to. It'd been hard enough to keep him out of her thoughts.

"I have his address. He lives in Wolffe Peak."

*Of course he does.* But speaking with him was the last thing Maddie wanted to do. Unfortunately, she had no choice in the matter. Legally, she had to seek him out. But when she was done with him, the man would be begging to sell her back his portion.

# ABOUT THE AUTHOR

Gwen Knight is a Canadian girl currently living in Jasper, AB. She graduated from the University of Lethbridge with a degree in Archaeology and Geography. Her interests consist of playing in the dirt, designing elaborate snow forts, boating, and archery.

## ALSO BY GWEN KNIGHT

*Wolffe Peak Series*
Reach for the Sky
Whispers in the Dark

*Blood Courtesan World*
Marked
Exposed — Coming Soon

*Harlequin Cravings*
Her Alpha Protector
A Hunter's Passion

*Cursed Holiday Series*
Death by Mistletoe
Death by Chocolate

*Isa Fae Collection*
Reaper

Printed in Great Britain
by Amazon